THE BAD GIRLS

Also By Bud Clifton

Let Him Go Hang
The Murder Specialist

THE BAD GIRLS

BUD CLIFTON

CUTTING EDGE

ISBN-13: 978-1-952138-78-2

Published by
Cutting Edge Books
PO Box 8212
Calabasas, CA 91372
www.cuttingedgebooks.com

CHAPTER ONE

TWO GIRLS sat in the back of the San Jose-San Francisco bus as though they were hiding. Nobody paid any attention to them, except for a boy who gave them the eye once in a while. The boy changed from stop to stop, but somehow it was always the same kind of boy. Apart from that they weren't noticeable girls. They looked clean, healthy and attractive, but they didn't look dangerous. They looked as though they'd never done anything worse in their lives than play kneesy in a soda fountain booth with the class president. They could have been any age from fifteen to twenty-one.

They were tired and dusty. They'd been traveling all day, for they'd come from Manteca, a town way down in the central section of California. Manteca wasn't much. It had a union high school, which is where the girls went, a movie house that only opened on Thursdays and Saturdays, and a sprinkling of stores against the barren yellow landscape. Perhaps it was the smallest town there ever was. But the girl sitting on the aisle didn't look like small town stuff. Her name was Allie. She was a violent blonde with a taut body and brittle bones. Her eyes were an honest blue. They were the only honest thing about her. She was nervous, yet completely at ease. As far as she was concerned, she wasn't running away. She was getting the hell out.

Janey was the one who was running away. Janey looked small town. She also looked nervous. She was small, and finely made, with a sensitive face and closely cut black hair. When she smiled she was delightful. She wasn't smiling now. Allie would never have left without her.

Boys of all ages go round in gangs, but nice girls go round in pairs. One is the leader and the other follows. They go through their whole lives like that. It was easy to tell that Allie was the leader here, and that was just the way she liked it.

The bus had choked up with exhaust fumes. Allie sat there in the half darkness looking straight in front of her, and wondering if Janey was really asleep, or just had her eyes shut. They had started out gaily, but now they were tired. They'd been riding in the bus all day. They felt clammy.

Allie was worried. She knew she'd have to get rid of Janey eventually, she always had known it, but it might not be so easy to do. But right now she needed her. It wouldn't do to let Janey get away. Not yet.

She smiled.

The bus roared along the bayshore highway, and lights flickered through the windows like glittering fish. On a bus you don't have to give any names, but they'd switched buses twice, just in case someone checked up. Now they had to switch again. For some reason this bus only went as far as Redwood City, which was thirty miles from San Francisco. They swung off the highway and up into the suburbs, and at last into the waiting room shed. The panel lights went on. The driver stood up and looked over the passengers.

"Redwood City," he said. "All out for changes to San Francisco."

Janey stirred and blinked her eyes. They got their luggage and got off. The night was cold. The station was really in the middle of nothing.

Allie watched Janey. She knew the signs. "You want to get off and run back," she said.

"No, I don't."

"Yes, you do. What do you think your folks would do to you back in that hick town?"

"I don't have any folks."

"What about that aunt of yours? She's your guardian, isn't she?"

Janey winced.

"She'd just show you the door without a 'by your leave,' and what would you do then? Work as a waitress at some cheap cafe, if you were lucky!"

"But how are we going to manage it?" asked Janey. She looked utterly lost.

Allie looked at her coolly. "I told you how we'll manage it."

"I don't want to do that."

"You wanted to do it all right back in Manteca. You thought it was a swell idea. I told you I'd let you have some money until we got started."

Janey looked suddenly curious. "But where did you get all that money?"

Allie shrugged. "It isn't so much. I worked." It was true. She had. It wasn't necessary to tell Janey at what, though. Besides she felt responsible for Janey. Sometimes Janey looked like a frightened mouse. It was hard to see how she'd gotten in this jam in the first place.

"Come on," she said gently. "I've always seen you through, haven't I?"

Janey nodded.

"It's going to be fun," Allie told her. "You never had so much fun. We'll really do something for a change, instead of just sit around all day. You'll see."

Janey looked down at her shoes. She had very small feet, with very delicate ankles. They were pretty. The trouble with her was she didn't realize just how pretty she was. Allie did. That's why Allie needed her along.

"I guess so," she said.

The bus came roaring round the corner of the depot and jerked into place. The sign said San Francisco Express. Janey looked at it dubiously.

"Come on, smile."

Janey smiled. It lit up her whole face. She had that gamin look. A gamin look went over big sometimes.

"That's better," said Allie. She picked up her suitcase and clicked over the cement towards the bus.

"I just got wobbly in the knees, I guess."

"Sure you did," soothed Allie. Her blue eyes softened. All the same she shepherded Janey ahead of her down the aisle, and she didn't really relax until the driver swung aboard and they were off to San Francisco non-stop.

Janey had her eyes shut. It was impossible to tell what she was thinking. Allie had known her ever since they were freshmen in high school, and she still didn't know.

That was in Manteca, too. It was awful to realize that neither of them had been out of Manteca in her whole life. But Janey seemed happy in Manteca. Allie could never make that out. Because she was part Portuguese, Janey didn't get many dates or anything like that. But she'd been happy. Now she was on the run.

Allie got a lot of dates. She got too many. Of course the really nice boys only met you on the sly, and if you couldn't land one of the nice boys by the time you graduated, there wasn't any point in staying in a place like Manteca at all.

In fact, if Janey hadn't just naturally gotten a crush on her the first day at High School, Allie couldn't have got through it. She'd have run away. The other girls thought they were so stuck up and know it all, and they'd been in Manteca since they were born. They had all the glamorpusses sewed up by the time they were nine.

Allie just had their pictures in her wallet. She got it out and flipped over the glassine envelopes, while Janey lay there with her eyes shut. There they all were, and she knew a lot about them. When she thought about that, it made her mad. She'd spent her life in Manteca practically, but because her folks had moved there when she was two, she didn't rate. She was too sophisticated. She came from the city.

She ran a finger over her lips and put the wallet away.

The bus passed San Francisco airport. They were getting closer. In the darkness the airport looked cold and glamorous, and a big four-engine plane circled down and zoomed over the highway.

All the same she wished there was someone waiting for them to tell them what to do. She wasn't as sure of herself as all that.

Beside her Janey stirred and said something in her sleep, and despite herself Allie felt grateful to have her along. She'd never have dared come alone. She knew that now. But Janey was such a silly, it sort of backed her up.

CHAPTER TWO

I T was maybe eight o'clock or eight-thirty. The bus had left the freeway and was running up through the slums towards town. It was a hot night. The air was sticky, but it had brought all the bums out. They moved around sluggishly, as though they had been sleeping all winter or were exploring the ocean floor. The neon signs shimmered in the haze. In order to get to the bus station the bus had to loop through the Civic Center.

Seen from five miles away, the city had seemed a magic place. Its pink glow lit up the sky. Its towers glittered against the stars. A searchlight cut up the heavens like a pie. Allie had been excited. As soon as she saw that agitated pink glow she had felt that everything would be all right.

Then the bus had dipped down into a big valley of white frame houses, and the vision had gotten lost. She didn't mind too much. She had to start somewhere. But the Civic Center depressed her. The Civic Center represented the law. It represented order and power. It made her wary. Then the bus crossed the garish main drag of Market Street and headed for the depot.

It looked fine to her. She saw the station looming up ahead.

No matter how many times the police raid them, bus stations are the same all over. This one was worse than most. It had all sorts of corners where things could happen. The passenger loading zone was a big low shed. It was always dusky in there. Pigeons flew in through the open doors and ran round among the cigarette stubs and the popcorn spilth. People waited round in tired attitudes. Some of them were even waiting for buses. On the other hand some of them didn't have anywhere else to sleep that night. Bus stations are always like that. The shore patrol sauntered in once or twice an evening. The military police followed them on the same route. The vice squad didn't bother to wear plain clothes. It just came in and plucked out its plum, like Jack Horner.

The bus drew in between the tall buildings, and the lights went on again. Allie woke up Janey. The two girls went down the aisle, lugging their suitcases. Nobody offered to help them. It wasn't that kind of a crowd.

Allie walked ahead. To look at her you'd have thought she knew exactly where she was going, and hadn't a worry in the world, but that would have been wrong. As soon as they came into the main waiting room, she knew how bewildered she felt. The full weight of the city dragged her down.

There was nothing furtive about that waiting room. It was a hustler's paradise, only without the hustlers, and neither one of the girls would have recognized a pimp if she saw one. It was the first time they'd ever seen the city on their own. Janey hung back a little and looked around her slowly.

Over on one side was a short order cafeteria. On the other the baggage room, a row of lockers, a counter where a guy sold identification bracelets, fatigue caps, and anything else a soldier could be talked into buying. The pinball machines were busy. So was the shoeshine stand.

"What do we do now? Where do we go?" asked Janey.

Allie didn't know. "We check the bags and look for a hotel. Then we pick them up."

"Can we get a room without a bag?"

"The sort of hotel we're going to we can," said Allie shortly. She led the way over to the baggage counter. Janey kept looking around her, as though she were afraid someone were following her. The baggage attendant grinned at them automatically. Janey looked pale.

"Well, what's wrong with you now?"

"Someone's watching us."

Allie shrugged. "So we're worth watching," she said. "I'm going to the john."

She wanted a moment to herself. She sauntered off to the ladies room, with her nose turned up in the air. But she could see plenty without looking, and she didn't like what she saw.

If she couldn't do better than this, she might just as well drop dead.

When she came back, at first she didn't see Janey. She wandered round the sleepy station, and found her behind the arrival and departure board, sitting down on the bench, staring at nothing, though plenty of people were staring at her, teenagers mostly, lined up at the ticket window with nothing else to stare at.

"We're being watched," said Janey.

"Where?"

"Over there."

Allie looked. He was a short, slim, dark man with hair like metal feathers and noticeable eyes. Her glance traveled past him, but she saw him all right.

"So what," she said. "Let's get going."

Janey got up uneasily. She stuck very close to Allie. Allie marched out of the building, and hesitating a moment, while the cab drivers came alert and then lapsed back into apathy, turned up towards Market Street.

"Is he still there?" she asked.

"I think so."

"Well look."

Janey looked. "I think he's following you."

"Well, well," said Allie. She walked a little faster, and Janey hurried to keep in step. There was a mirror column in a clothing store, and Allie caught sight of him behind them.

"What a nerve," she said.

"Suppose he's a cop," said Janey softly, clutching her purse.

Allie sniffed. "He's not a cop. He's just hungry," she told her. "Besides, we haven't done anything."

"We ran away."

"We didn't run away. We just left. Besides, I don't think your aunt has any bulletins out, and my folks wouldn't have either. If you could call them folks."

Janey was hurt by that. She shut up. They came to the stop sign on the corner. Market Street stretched before them both ways. It was cheap and dirty and glittering, and everybody who didn't have anything else to do was idling up and down it.

"Is he still following us?" asked Allie.

"I think so."

"Huh," said Allie. The signal changed and they crossed the street. On the other side Allie turned left, so she could look back. He was there all right, on the curb they had left, but he made no move to follow them. She felt vaguely annoyed.

He looked after them. His name was Torrey, and he was twenty-four. Allie had been wrong about one thing. He *was* a cop. He was attached to the vice squad. He wasn't working that night, though. He'd just gone by the bus station on the off chance that his partner, Sanducci, might be there and would maybe have a cup of coffee. Sanducci was not there, and that had left him at a loose end.

Janey had caught his eye and fascinated him. Not having anything else to do, and not meaning anything in particular by it, he had trailed them to the corner.

He saw them pause on the farther curb, and guessed they knew he had been following them. Girls always knew these things. He was shy. He wasn't going to make any effort. But the small dark girl he'd remember. He didn't know why. There weren't many girls he remembered, but when one did catch his eye, he never forgot her. He was a lonely man. When he saw a girl like that, he thought about her a lot.

Right now, though, he tried to shrug it off. Teenage girls weren't part of his job. His job was watching Sanducci. And he wasn't really making a career of the Vice Squad either. That was just a blind.

CHAPTER THREE

JANEY hurried to keep up with Allie. She had never been in a big town before. She looked straight ahead of her and didn't like what she saw.

The tenderloin of any city is pretty grim. The Tenderloin of San Francisco was pie-shaped, and ran over hilly ground to Market Street. It was wedged between the Civic Center and the smart section of town.

Allie seemed to know where she was going. She marched up Market Street, pretending not to notice anything, but knowing very well she was noticeable. So was Janey, but Janey didn't like being noticeable. She was relieved when Allie turned off Market and up into the hotel quarter. It was a landscape of bars, neon signs, and tall, bay-windowed resident apartments. At least they were called resident apartments. The region was dingy and dirty, but somehow the air was cleaner than it had been on Market.

"Won't they ask about baggage?" asked Janey.

"You naïve or something?"

Janey knew better than to ask anything else. When Allie was worried or upset, she had a bad temper. She had a special smile at times like that, and the smile was terrible.

Allie wanted something half way between a flea-bag and the Ritz. It took her a while to find it.

The first hotel didn't have a vacancy. In other words it turned them down. That made Allie mad. The second one wasn't so particular.

It was called *The Florida*. Allie marched right in. The lobby was white tile with some beat up rugs for the sake of appearances. It had one rickety elevator and a desk clerk who had seen everything and didn't know a thing.

"You'll want two rooms," he said. He looked them up and down and seemed less bored.

Janey blushed.

"Any luggage?"

"It's at the bus depot."

"Hmmm," said the clerk. "Staying long?"

"A couple of weeks."

He raised his eyebrows. "O. K. sister, if you say so."

"I'm not your sister," said Allie, being real haughty.

"We'll see," said the clerk. He shot her a quick look. "That'll be a week in advance, for both of you."

"That's crazy."

"You want the rooms, don't you?"

Allie glared at him and paid up. He handed over the keys. "You want to go up now?" he asked.

Allie didn't answer. She marched over to the elevator. It took a while to come. They stood with their back to the desk, but Janey was conscious of the desk clerk behind them. He seemed to think it was a good joke or something.

The elevator came down, and they bumped up in it to the fourth floor. The corridor was dark and dreary. It hadn't been painted for years. Their rooms were at the front. Janey was sure they were being watched.

"Of course we are," said Allie. "It's that kind of hotel." Behind them a door closed softly. The place was restless. There was a funny smell in the air. Allie put the key into the door of number fifteen and shoved it open. They went inside.

Janey looked round in dismay. It wasn't what you'd call homey. There was no bathroom. The bathroom was down the hall. The floor was linoleum fifty years old, with sprays of diseased yellow ferns half rubbed away on a green ground. There was a cheap rug and a washstand in the corner. She couldn't keep her eyes off the washstand. The bed was ugly and hard, the bureau yellow pine, and the chair was motheaten mohair. There was one picture on the wall. It showed a black wolf in blue white snow and it was called *The Lone Wolf.* The curtains were held together chiefly by their own dirt. She went over and looked out the bay window, into the street below.

Next to her was a neon sign. A pink neon girl eight feet high kicked a ball. She had three white legs for the neon to run through, and the ball wound up in a martini glass. The ball was green. Across the street was another bay-windowed hotel. On the third floor opposite a woman with fallen breasts and a henna rinse was shaving her arms slowly and painfully. Janey let the curtain fall.

Allie had been watching her.

"We'd better go get the bags," she said. She looked round the room. "Cheer up. We won't be in this dump for the rest of our lives."

"We haven't much cash."

"We'll have more," said Allie and smirked.

They went back to the bus station. The man who had been watching them wasn't there. Then they went back to the hotel. Janey's room was just like Allie's. There was a connecting door between them, but it was locked. She heard Allie go down the hall to the shower, and lay down on the bed, shutting her eyes.

She wanted to cry.

The sound of the shower stopped. She lay there listening to Allie whistle while she dressed. Then there was a knock on her door. She didn't answer it. She didn't unlock the door either. Her body tensed.

The connecting door rattled, the bolt shot, and Allie stood in the doorway. She was wearing a fawn tailored suit to make her look older, and she had combed out her blond hair, which was clipped short to her head, like an Italian movie star.

"O.K.," she began. "Let's get going." Then she stopped. "You aren't even dressed."

"Couldn't we just stay here tonight?"

"If you think I'm going to stay in this dump you're crazy," said Allie. She sat down on the bed. "What's the matter, you got cold feet?"

Janey looked at her and then nodded.

"You have to start sometime."

"But not now."

"You're scared," said Allie contemptuously, perhaps because she was scared herself. "Come on." She held out her hand.

Janey turned on her side.

"You know why you're here. Sulking in your room isn't going to pay the rent. Or the other thing."

"What other thing?"

"You know what other thing," said Allie. She took out a nail file and went to work on her nails.

Janey did know what other thing. She stared at the linoleum by the bed. The scuffled ferns looked like octopus tentacles. She got up and went to the shower. When she got back Allie was still filing her nails. She went right on filing them until Janey was ready.

"That's better," she said, but she sounded mad. "I'm not going to be your meal ticket forever. For a meal ticket you need a man." Keeping Janey in front of her, she went down the corridor towards the elevators. To look at her anyone would have thought she knew what she was doing.

As they went by the desk, the clerk looked up with a knowing smirk. As far as he was concerned, his judgment had been vindicated. Allie stuck her tongue out at him, and he looked down again at his comic book.

CHAPTER FOUR

THEY sauntered down to Market Street, looking in the shop windows, but heading towards the upper end. It was ten o'clock.

Every city has a Market Street, a sort of main line to the sewers. No matter what it was once, one look, and you know what it is now.

Beyond the bus station around the corner, and on the other side, it opened out into the tail end of the Civic Center. This was its toughest spot. It was a tangle of cheap stores, pick-up bars, penny arcades, greasy restaurants, and triple feature movie houses. Every gang hangs out on its own corner. The gang here was randy and rowdy. There was a posse of teenage would-be toughs, lolling against the walls, with their thumbs stuck in their pants. Most of them had Mexican or Portuguese blood. There were a few Greeks. The older motorcycle gang hung out here, too. They hunched over the coffee bars, wasted time on the pin-ball machines, or strutted up and down the street. Part of the time they were cruising, part of the time they weren't, but they were always ready for something to happen. It was a weird crowd but it was young. The creepy older ones couldn't stand the pace. They lurked farther downtown.

Because it was all out in the hard neon glare, the police didn't bother it much. Even to Janey it was sort of exciting. She'd never seen so many people in one place before. There weren't any cat-calls, but they did get an occasional whistle. Allie loitered along, walking on the inside. She hadn't quite learned how to walk in high heels yet. That gave her the wobble of a horse on stilts. She didn't want to show it, but she was nervous. Besides, she was someone who stood out. No matter what she did, people would always notice her.

They passed a clump of kids on a corner, leaning against the wall of a drugstore, not doing anything in particular. They were a tight little unit, you could see that at once. They sort of stood out. There were eight of them. Six of them were motorcycle toughs, all in the same gang. Allie didn't think much of them. She went by with her nose in the air.

There was a movement along the wall as they shifted position.

"Hey, get that," said one of them. He had a high piping baby voice.

"Yeah, I got it," said Purvis, the leader of the gang. On their backs they wore round yellow circles of felt with black wasps stamped on them. Purvis was wearing white peg pants, a purple shirt with the collar turned up, and heavy loafers. He had a dreamy, dangerous face, long sideburns that splayed out in front, and black wavy hair. The pupils of his eyes were small. His body was tight and wild, as though he couldn't keep it still. He snapped his fingers.

"They must be new."

"Yeah," said Purvis. "They look new."

"I could go for that," said Eddie, the one with the thin voice.

"You ain't going for nothing," said Purvis. His eyes followed the girls as they walked down the street, and he eased himself away from the wall. "Come on," he said.

"Why?"

"We haven't anything to lose." He looked around. "I said, come on. I want to see what happens next."

"Nothing happens next."

"Didn't you ever follow a pigeon?" asked Purvis. "It just drives them nuts."

The eight of them spread out around the sidewalk and ambled up the street after the girls. Purvis' eyes glittered, but he wasn't in any hurry. He was thinking things over. In their boots the others made a racket. The sidewalk wasn't that wide either. He grinned. The girls were getting nervous.

He slouched along, with his thumbs in his pockets, chewing his gum, and feeling fine.

Janey felt her ears burn. She started to walk faster.

It seemed to annoy Allie, too. "Is that creep still behind us?" she asked.

Janey looked over her shoulder. Purvis grinned at her and waggled his hips. That creep still was.

"We'll lose him," said Allie. "He probably doesn't have the price of a drink. We can't walk Market Street all night, anyhow."

They had come to a bar in the middle of the block. It had a glass front painted black, so that nothing could be seen from the street. It was called the Jickey Club. Maybe instinct had taken Allie there. Maybe somebody had told her about it once. With Allie it would be hard to tell.

She pushed open the door and went inside. Janey followed her. On the door was a sign saying the bar was off bounds to military personnel. The sign had old-fashioned scare lettering. It looked like a nineteenth century warning against cholera.

The bar was very dim, and what light there was was pink. It was crowded. For the first time Allie seemed ill at ease. Then she moved through the crowd, towards the booths at the back, which were even darker.

One of the bartenders looked up. His hands hesitated slightly, drying a glass, and then he glanced towards the door. The door opened again. Purvis and his gang came into the room in a wedge. Purvis winked at the bartender.

Allie slid into one of the booths, and Janey sat down opposite her. Now that she was sitting down, Allie had gotten her self-possession back. She began to look around her with bright, curious eyes.

The joint was certainly crowded. There were five or six bar girls. Allie didn't think much of them. They were too old, and they had hard skins. They looked as though they had been born in their cocktail dresses. But she watched them carefully. She wanted to see how it was done. It fascinated her.

Most of the customers looked either flashy or tough, but there was a sprinkling of tired businessmen. It was one of those places where so much is happening at once that nothing seems to be happening at all.

The B-girls had a fine relaxed attitude. They made more out of the drinks than they did out of taking the customer home for a quiet half-hour, and their own drinks were mostly water. They didn't have to worry about getting drunk. Besides the light was kind to them. In a business like that, the older you get, the darker you like your places.

"Where is he?" asked Janey, in a frightened voice.

"Where's who?"

"That man."

"I don't know." Clearly Allie didn't want anything to do with Purvis. Purvis didn't come up to her standards. But she knew he was there all right. He was leaning by the door, with his gang around him, just watching idly, and playing with something in his pocket. The place was beginning to get busier. Every time the door opened Purvis would turn round and nod. There was something snakelike about him. Despite herself she watched him.

He went over to the bar and spoke to the bartender. The bartender seemed flustered, and nodded towards the back of the room warningly. Purvis frowned, shoved his hands in his pockets, started back towards the rear booths, and then changed his mind.

He went back to his gang. Allie caught a phrase about honest cops. "He'll loosen up. They all do," said Purvis. His voice was furry and babyish and urgent. You couldn't quite make out the words, but they went right through you.

Allie looked the other way. There was a man sitting at the middle of the bar, and she knew she'd caught his eye. He wasn't a very nice man. He had salesman written all over him, and he was real rabbity. He had a moon face, and a moon-shaped body, and tiny little boneless hands and feet. Just to be sporty, he was wearing black loafers with tassels and a rumpled brown suit with a pale red glen plaid. He had a moustache, and his eyes were bright little black pebbles. He had been glancing her way for some time.

Allie sniffed, took out a compact, and powdered her nose. She was getting thirsty. There didn't seem to be anybody waiting on anybody at all.

Allie looked at him in the mirror of her compact. It seemed to her that she could do better than that. There was something wrong with the guy. She couldn't put her finger on it, but she could sense it. He was beginning to give her the creeps. All the same she looked up and smiled at him. She had to begin somewhere.

The fat man downed his drink and put his hands on the bar, ready to get up, his eyes watching the booth in the mirror behind the bar. The bartender slid down towards him.

"Have another on the house," he suggested.

The man looked up sharply. "Why?"

"We've got guests." The bartender nodded towards the far booth. In it were two men.

The fat man shrugged. "They're always here. What do you pay protection for?"

"One of them's Torrey. He's new. He hasn't gotten the idea yet." The bartender stared at him. "You don't want to go monkeying round with that sort of stuff."

"No, I guess I don't. Not yet anyway."

"We'll see," said the bartender. "We don't want another suspension, or anything like that."

The fat man sat where he was. Allie relaxed. She still hadn't gotten served. But something told her not to go up to the bar. Besides, a girl shouldn't have to pay for her own drinks. At the same time she knew something had gone wrong. She hadn't missed a thing. She didn't like anything to go wrong in front of Janey. Janey was hard enough to keep under control as it was.

The air was heavy and stale. It stank of liquor and cheap perfume and sweaty clothes. Suddenly the juke box stopped. Purvis slouched out from the wall and started down the length of the room. Allie watched him. She couldn't help it. In his own cheap way Purvis was the sort of person women always watched. He had glamour. It didn't make any difference that he knew it.

At the end of the room was a small bandstand. Three men had come out of a side door. They were a jazz combo. They wore slacks and blue sportshirts open at the neck with big Hawaiian flowers all over them. One of them handed Purvis a black steel guitar.

Purvis preened himself. If he had a weak spot, this was it. He fiddled with the microphone, sliding it up to the right height. The public address system wasn't any good anyway. It was just there to keep the cops away; if a bar had a floorshow it didn't get raided quite so often. So bars like this served up a floorshow the way other bars always kept a tin of soup behind the bar, to prove they served food, which is what they had to do according to the California licensing laws.

Then Purvis tore loose. Allie didn't want anything to do with him, but right then she got in over her depth. He was real gone. He was agonizing. He threw himself into a song, and it sounded as though someone were plucking a short-haired cat. His smooth baby face puckered up and he threw his body around, and did everything with that guitar except eat it.

He had a funny voice, too. It was half Negro and half Okie. It was all covered with caterpillars, and it sort of ate you away. For a moment Allie forgot where she was or what she had come for.

She leaned forward, peering out of the booth at him. He didn't notice her or anything else. He was inside the song. He had his eyes closed. It was like an orgasm.

Nobody else at the bar seemed to pay much attention. A girl came in the door, though, and leaned against it, listening. She looked about eighteen, but there was something about her that set her off from everybody else. Allie could see there was some sort of connection between her and Purvis, and she didn't like it. For some reason that girl made her shrink up inside herself. As soon as she saw her she was afraid of her.

She couldn't tell why. Purvis's gang was saying hello to her. Her name was Vera. And Allie didn't like Vera at all. Vera made her skin crawl. Yet Vera was only a teenage Italian with that lean, tight almost Chinese face that North Italians have sometimes. But there was something about the way Vera moved and looked that was frightening. And Vera knew it, too. She glanced towards the booth and then moved towards Purvis. She looked annoyed.

Purvis opened his eyes, reached the end of his song, and looked at Vera. He just looked. Slowly he put down the guitar.

Vera smiled at him. And right then Allie knew that he was afraid of Vera, too. Of course he wouldn't admit it and he wouldn't show it, but he was. He jumped down from the bandstand, and the two of them stood there talking. Purvis glanced rapidly over towards their booth. He caught Allie staring right at him. She flushed and looked down. He seemed worried. He talked rapidly to Vera. But whatever he was saying, Vera wasn't having any of it. She turned and walked away from him, sauntering over to the bar, where she tapped the fat salesman on the shoulder and whispered something to him before she drifted on down the bar. She came to roost at the very end of it, where she sat quietly watching the room. The bartender brought her a drink without even being asked.

The fat man and one of the B-girls had finally gotten together. They left the bar and came over and sat in the booth behind Allie's. She could hear them murmuring.

So far Janey hadn't said a word. But she looked pale. It got on Allie's nerves.

"Why don't you relax?" she said. "How are you ever going to get anybody that way? You look like a frightened mouse or something."

Janey drew back against the booth wall. "Everybody's watching us," she said.

"So what? We're new."

"It's the way they watch us. As though they weren't. As though they were going to do something to us."

"Well, what do you think we're here for?"

Janey flushed. "That's not what I mean."

"You're so scared you don't know what you mean."

"Aren't you?"

"No," said Allie, and felt the pit of her stomach contract.

"Oh, let's not fight," said Janey impatiently.

"Who's fighting?"

For a moment Allie had stopped watching the room. Now someone was standing in front of their booth, and she looked up unwillingly. It was Purvis, standing with his feet planted apart, and his thumbs in the loops of his belt. He was being Western now. He looked as though he had all sorts of parts for himself to play. She winced and he grinned at her.

"You girls must be getting sort of thirsty," he said. "You've been sitting here quite a while."

Allie relaxed. "We sure are," she said, gave him a dazzling smile, and waited for him to sit down. He didn't sit down however, and over his shoulder she could see Vera at the bar, watching.

"That's a shame, because you aren't going to get a thing," he said. He leaned over the table. "You girls from the police, or something?"

Janey shifted uneasily.

"It could be a frame, it's been known," he said. "Let's see your identity cards."

"What identity cards?"

"Something that proves you're old enough to drink. Or do anything else for that matter."

Allie reached for her purse, but he grabbed her hand. "You haven't got any," he said. He glanced towards the rear booths. "You wouldn't know the gentlemen back there, by any chance."

"We just got here," said Allie nervously. She didn't want Janey throwing hysterics.

"Maybe you should just quietly leave," said Purvis.

"It's a free world."

"You think so?"

"You the bouncer or something?"

"Yeah, I'm the bouncer. Also something," he said. He just stood there and waited. Allie hissed, and gathered up her purse.

"That's right," he said, "just you come right along."

"I guess he means it," said Allie. "But we won't forget it." She motioned Janey to get up. She could feel herself blushing. Together the two girls moved towards the door, with Purvis right behind them. Vera watched them, and smiled nastily at the bartender. It didn't make Allie feel any better.

"Anyone would think I was a child," she said.

"That's just what we were afraid of," Purvis told her. It drew a big laugh from his gang near the door.

CHAPTER FIVE

THE TWO MEN in the back booth were Torrey and Sanducci. This was one of Sanducci's regular places to kill a few hours on his beat, and as far as he knew Torrey was just a new cop waiting to learn the angles. That was the way Torrey wanted him to look at it, anyhow. Sanducci was a dangerous man. The District Attorney had made that very clear. If Torrey got caught, anything might happen to him, and the D.A.'s office wouldn't back him up. It could hardly be expected to. It had to hide it's hand, otherwise Sanducci might be even harder to catch than he was already.

But so far there didn't seem to have been a leak. Sanducci even seemed to like him. Not that he was telling him anything he didn't know, but then if the D.A. was right about Sanducci, Sanducci wouldn't tip his hand for quite a while.

The girls made a noise getting up. Sanducci leaned out of the booth just in time to see them leave. So did Torrey, and recognized Janey at once. Sanducci noticed that.

"Anyone you know?" he asked.

"No," Torrey told him. He didn't know why, but something told him to shut up.

All the same he was disappointed. He had liked the dark one, and they certainly hadn't wasted any time. He wondered who had passed them on to Purvis. He didn't wonder why. They had a fine little file on Purvis down at headquarters, though they hadn't been able to get him on anything yet.

"Nuts," said Sanducci. "We aren't doing ourselves any good here. Let's move on." He got up.

Purvis waited until they had passed, and then started towards the door himself, followed by his boys. But he didn't want the boys along right now. He told them to stay at the Jickey.

Vera watched him.

"Where do you think you're going?" she asked.

"Out for a walk."

"Yeah," said Vera. "I'll bet." She nodded over his head. "Take Pedersen with you."

"Why should I?"

"He might keep you out of trouble. He's your friend, isn't he?"

"So he says," said Purvis. He hesitated, irritated with her. "Okay, if you say so."

He cocked an eyebrow at Pedersen, and the two of them went out the door.

"Quail," said Pedersen chattily. He was a short, dark boy with black eyes, his torso swamped in a heavy and beat up leather jacket. But he was good to have around. He was the one who ran errands and really moved the stuff around. He was raunchy, too. He was the only one of the bunch that Purvis trusted. They'd gone to school together, and stolen their first car together, too, if it came to that.

"Vera doesn't like this," said Pedersen. "I guess you know that."

"Vera's nuts." Purvis looked up and down the street. The girls had maybe three minutes start. It made them a little hard to spot. But they weren't city girls. They had a different way of walking. He saw them soon enough. "Where do you think they're headed," he asked.

"Hotel probably."

"Maybe," said Purvis. "Let's go see."

Away from Vera he felt better. It wasn't that Vera could do anything to him. He could get rid of her any time he wanted to. But somehow he never got around to it, even if she did make him look like a fool.

The girls were walking rapidly. Anyone would have thought they knew where they were going. Purvis had to admit that Allie had a provocative butt. She wriggled it all over the place, and it began to fascinate him. But he wasn't in any hurry to catch up.

They stopped for a stoplight, and Purvis drew back into the shelter of a store. When he came out on the street again, they had turned off Market up into the Tenderloin.

"Do you think they're going where I think they're going," asked Pederson. "Or is it just instinct?"

Purvis shrugged.

"They're so wet behind the ears they don't know what they're doing," he said. But he began to walk a little faster.

On the corner was a brightly lit ice cream parlor. It had a u-shaped counter, a juke box, and a greenish fluorescent light. It was deserted now, but it would start to fill up again around two A.M. It was called Bob and Anna's. There really was a Bob and an Anna. They were a sleek couple in their thirties, and through Vera, Purvis knew all about them. They just couldn't have been any nicer, and they had a shocking pink Cadillac convertible with black leather upholstery and a weekend cottage over in Sausolito, across the Bay, where the parties were really wild. The ice cream parlor was a front for teen-age call house vice. They were shrewd about it, too. So far the police hadn't caught on at all.

Allie and Janey headed right for it.

"It could be coincidence, but I don't think so," said Pedersen. "They must have met a traveling salesman and heisted his address book."

Purvis laughed.

"You want to go in?"

"In a minute. There isn't any rush." Purvis stood watching them through the glass, while they sat down, settled themselves, and ordered.

"Well my goodness," he said. "Banana splits. Okay. Let's go in. It's getting cold out here."

Pedersen shoved open the door, and they went inside. Purvis waved to Anna who smiled back, but watched Pedersen with a worried expression. She didn't trust Pedersen much. Purvis sat down next to Allie and let Pedersen fall into place beside him.

Allie gave him a furtive look and popped a gob of fake cream into her mouth. Purvis gave her time to swallow it.

"I guess you thought I was real mean," he said. "I mean back there."

"I didn't think about you at all," said Allie. She stuck her nose up into the air.

Purvis laughed, and twisted on his stool. He didn't seem to mind a bit.

"You girls know what you're doing?" he asked.

"What do you think?"

"I don't think. There isn't any money in it. Only maybe somebody might have told you the heat was on. If they told you where to go and all, they could at least have told you that."

"Nobody told us anything."

"Really?"

"We were just walking around."

Anna was fussing with the silex machine. But she was taking in every word. That didn't bother Purvis a bit. Allie was all right. Allie was the sort of girl he understood. But the thin dark one puzzled him.

"How old are you?" he asked.

"That's none of your business."

"Under the limit?"

Allie hesitated, seemed to make up her mind, and then nodded. Despite herself her left hand was sort of oozing over towards his thigh. It amused him. She was a real bitch, and she looked so innocent too.

"Got any money?" he asked.

"Not for you." Allie instantly looked suspicious.

"Finish up and let's get out of here."

"Why should I?"

"It isn't a good place for you to be," he said. He winked. "What you need is an identity card. Something to prove you're of age, see what I mean? Otherwise nobody would touch you. Not with a ten foot pole."

Allie looked as though she was going to climb on her high horse and get indignant. But then she changed her mind.

"That woman back at the club, she was your girl," she said, "Wasn't she?"

"Maybe she thinks she is."

Allie relaxed. "You could introduce us to your friend," she said. "Where do we get these cards?"

"I know a place."

"Where?"

"I'll take you there tomorrow. It wouldn't be open now." Purvis eased himself off his stool. Anna was staring at him, and he gave her an okay sign. She looked relieved. Pedersen held the door open, and they all went out into the street again.

Once more Allie seemed a little uncertain. Then she headed right for the hotel. It was only around the block. The four of them walked in silence, Allie and Purvis ahead. Janey couldn't think of anything to say to Pedersen. She only knew she didn't want to be paired off with him, if that was what Allie had in mind. The whole idea made her panic.

She thought maybe Purvis would say something about the hotel. She was ashamed of staying at a hotel like that, and Purvis would be the one to notice that, not Pedersen. But he didn't. They crossed the lobby. It was deserted. The desk clerk didn't even bother to look up. He seemed to take it for granted they'd come back with a couple of men. Janey winced.

They reached the elevator, and waited for it to come down. It seemed ages before it settled into place and the doors swung open. Janey bolted inside, turned round, and faced the others. Pedersen looked puzzled.

Purvis took Allie's arm.

"You can't come up," said Allie.

Purvis let go. He was still being amused, but his eyes weren't amused.

"You know what you're here for, don't you?" he asked. "Or do you mean maybe I don't understand?"

"Not now," said Allie, but she made some sort of gesture towards him, that Janey couldn't catch.

"Oh I see," said Purvis grandly, and glanced rapidly at Pedersen. "Excuse me." His eyes passed curiously over Janey, and then he turned away.

The doors shut and they went up in the elevator to their floor.

"The nerve of him," said Allie. She looked guilty. "Who does he think he is?"

They got out and walked down the hall to their rooms. Janey wanted to stay with Allie, but Allie wouldn't let her. So she went to her own room. She lay there in the darkness for a long time, unable to sleep, and pretending to herself that she was sleeping. That was a trick she had learned at home. At last she heard footsteps coming down the corridor, and the creak of a door, and it was almost as though that was what she had been waiting for. She turned over with a sob after that and went right to sleep.

When she woke up it was broad daylight and somebody was pounding on her door. She tightened the cord on her pajamas and ran to the door. She thought it was Allie. It wasn't Allie. It was Purvis. He hadn't changed and he hadn't shaved, but he had so little beard that it was scarcely noticeable. He seemed pretty cheerful.

"Come on. Hop into some clothes. We've got things to do," he said. He was quite nonchalant about it.

She did as she was told. But she had to close the door in his face, for he was still standing there.

"You're a strange one," he said, but he let her do it.

She put on a summer print and knocked on the door of Allie's room. When she went in Purvis was leaning against the window, looking out into the street, and Allie looked mad. Not that she wasn't smiling and everything, but Janey had known Allie a long time. She could recognize the signs.

Purvis treated them to breakfast. He was in a real good mood. They went to Bob and Anna's. Apparently that was where he always went. No doubt they were expected to go there too. Janey didn't like the place. She particularly didn't like Anna's looks. But the food was fine.

"This place we're going to might maybe surprise you a little," said Purvis. He didn't pay the check. He told Anna to put it on the tab. After all, he was a big wheel. He made that quite clear.

They left the cafe. Purvis and Allie walked ahead. Purvis walked rapidly, and Janey couldn't catch up with them. She was puzzled. She felt shut out. It was as though Allie and Purvis knew something that she didn't.

Purvis paused on a corner and again began to walk rapidly.

"I thought we were going for the cards," complained Allie. She didn't trust him.

"We are. I gotta see Eddie first."

"Who's Eddie?"

"Eddie Pedersen. The guy with us last night. He's a friend of mine. He does what I tell him to."

They went to the block on Market where the Civic Center opened out into the street. There was a row of tattoo parlors, greasy spoons, and dark bars there. Purvis seemed to be timing himself pretty closely. He wasn't anxious or in a hurry or anything, but he glanced at the neon clocks in the bar windows. He reached the end of the block and stopped.

"What do we do now?" asked Allie. She sounded impatient.

"Now we wait," said Purvis. He seemed to have his mind on other things.

They didn't have to wait long. Pedersen came down the side street on a red servicycle and pulled in to the curb. He was wearing black jeans and a plaid shirt, and he looked cheerful.

"How did it go?" asked Purvis.

"It went okay." Pedersen glanced rapidly at the girls.

"Delivering any films?"

Again Pedersen glanced at the girls. He seemed uncertain. "Some." he said shortly. He raced the engine.

"Go over to Pop's," said Purvis. "We gotta get the girls cards. Everything okay at Pops?"

"As far as I know."

"You get rid of the other stuff?"

Pedersen nodded.

Purvis seemed relieved. "Hand it over," he said. Pedersen shrugged, zipped open a pocket on his shirt, and handed over a roll of bills. Then he made a u-turn, went ahead of them along Market, drew the servicycle up on the sidewalk, cut the engine, and waited for them. Purvis ambled towards him, counting the money. Allie watched the money. Janey watched Pedersen.

When they drew abreast of him, Pedersen dismounted and lounged ahead of them into a pinball alley. It was called *Fun Street,* and that was what it was, an open arcade lined with the sort of things people do to fill in time. There were about ten gaudy pin-ball machines, several 'photograph yourself' booths, a mechanical fortune-teller, and a tattoo shack, plastered with designs, and a plate glass window to watch through. It was empty. There was an out-of-town newspaper rack, a cigarette and candy counter, and a shoeshine stand. At this hour of the morning the place was pretty deserted. Purvis seemed to know the way. So did Pedersen. They walked straight through to the back, into a room marked private, which was used for storage, and down a flight of stairs to the basement. There was a scuttling down below them. Purvis just yelled "Pop," and the scuttling stopped.

They halted at the bottom of the stairs. The cellar was dim, and stacked high with boxes. There was a smooth clicking noise, which came from a movie projector propped on a packing case. In fact, part of the room was made up to resemble an interior, open at one end. The projector faced a screen. It was a sound film. From the track came strange gasps and moans. The sound track was not very good, and buzzed and hissed under the sounds. Janey followed the beam of light to the screen, and jerked violently, scarcely able to believe what she saw. Then with a snarl the film ended, at the end of the reel, in a meaningless rush of symbols and sounds, and the screen went white.

The old man hunched over the projector straightened up. He was about forty, with a tight, lined, bad-tempered face and lustreless eyes. No matter how often he washed he would always look dirty.

"That the new one, Pop?" asked Pedersen.

"Part of it," said Pop shortly.

"Going out tonight?"

Pop scuttled away from the projector. "Club out in the Mission wants it," he said. He saw the girls. "You've no business bringing chippies down here. Get them out."

Allie looked angry.

"You shouldn't watch your own films so much, Pop," said Purvis. "It gives you ideas. These are real respectable girls. They just lost all their identity cards, that's all. They're thirsty and they need a drink."

"You shouldn't bring them down here. How do I know who they are? I can see *what* they are, though."

Janey blushed.

Purvis stared at Pop. "It's a job," he said. "It pays cash. You want it or you don't want it?"

Pop spat. He leaned forward, and his eyes caught Janey's ankles, and then moved up slowly over her body. He had the sort of eyes that touch you all over.

"You ever pose for stills?" he asked. "You'd look good in stills, and there's money in them."

Janey had never seen anything like that film before, but she knew what she had seen. She just stared at him.

"Cut the comedy, Pop," said Purvis. He went over and looked at the labels on a stack of film cans. "Just think what they pay for this stuff, when they could do it for free," he said.

"You put them down."

"Okay. I wasn't hurting anything," said Purvis.

Pedersen slapped the projector affectionately, and chuckled. "I'd better get out. I got deliveries to make." he said. "One way and another."

Purvis looked at him angrily.

"Film I mean." Pedersen scooped up the film cans, and held them against his chest. "Okay Pop?"

Pop nodded and led the way towards the stairs, under which he had a desk. Purvis nudged the girls forward after him, while Pedersen clattered up the stairs in his heavy boots.

Pop sat down on the desk, put his glasses on, and peered at Allie and Janey. "Well, well," he said. "Now what do you suppose the traffic will bear?"

"Go easy, they're friends of mine," said Purvis.

"Both of them? Already? You should work so fast!" Pop sighed and pulled open a drawer beside him. It contained several cardboard boxes. "Do they want their own names? That would cost them more."

"It doesn't matter."

Pop shrugged. "It's a pity, but they all learn fast," he said. "And you teach them. What I want to know is, how did you get that way so young."

"I met you," said Purvis.

Pop chuckled. "Yeah, I guess you did, at that. Not that you haven't a racket of your own, or two." He looked up shrewdly. "One of these days you'll branch out right into the local precinct station. The trouble with you is, you're overeager."

"The trouble with me is you haven't a thing on me."

"I can wait," said Pop. He was opening the cardboard boxes. "We can't make them too old," he said. "They don't look it." He fished out a couple of driving licenses.

"What about their prints?"

"Nobody's going to check their prints unless they're hauled in," said Pop placidly. "Gloria Applegate and Rose Pledger," he read. "I guess you're going to have to be Rose." He nodded at Janey. "You're the dark one."

"Hand them over," said Purvis.

"They're going to need some other stuff. Now if they were boys, they'd be set. I have a fine bunch of draft cards. Women are harder."

Purvis handed the girls the cards. "How much?"

"Fifteen each," said Pop cautiously.

"Ten," said Allie abruptly. Her eyes hadn't missed a thing in that cellar.

Pop looked amused. "Fifteen."

Purvis scowled. "The lady said ten."

"The lady! Well, for friends I make a special rate. Ten, and I hope they drop dead." Pop watched while Allie dug into her purse and paid for both of them. He didn't miss the meaning of that, and his eyes were on Janey. He folded the bills out lovingly and put them in his wallet. "Well Rose," he said to Janey, "if you ever run out on them and need a little cash, look me up. We could make some really beautiful stills. Beautiful."

"She's not going anywhere, Pop."

"Of course not. Do they ever? But they think they are," Pop told him. He looked beyond Purvis towards the projector, wistfully.

"I'd sure hate to keep you from reel two," Purvis told him. He stood up, and took Allie's arm. "Let's blow," he said. "I don't know how you stand it down here, with all this fresh air and all."

Pop shrugged. "It suits me."

As they went up the stairs, Janey could feel the old man's eyes running over her bottom and her legs. It made her walk tightly. They went out through the back alley and stood blinking in the brighter light of the street. It was ten-thirty.

"He gives me the creeps," said Allie.

"Pop's clever," said Purvis. "He's a real character." He looked at his watch. "You girls better go rest or do some shopping or something," he said. "I've got things to do. Nothing happens round here until about ten anyway. I'll pick you up tonight and put the guys down at the club wise."

"You're going to see Vera," said Allie. Vera was the girl at the club.

"Vera and I have known each other a long time, honey," said Purvis. "Now don't you go carrying on."

Neither one of them paid any attention to Janey. Purvis hesitated, and then took off down the street. He looked real jaunty and he seemed to know where he was going. Allie looked after him.

Janey just had to know. "You've been with him," she said. It made her feel scared.

"One of these days you're going to make me feel tired," said Allie shortly. She glanced after Purvis again, and then straightened up. "You've gotta do a lot of crumby things sometimes. And once we're in at the club, maybe things will be different, who knows? We got the cards, didn't we?"

Janey still held hers in her hand. She looked down at it. It said she was Rose Pledger. She was twenty-two. She came from Modesto, she had black hair and blue eyes, she was single, and she weighed a hundred and six pounds and was five feet four. Actually she was five feet five and a half and weighed a hundred and ten. But that didn't seem to make any difference. The thumb print on the license was smudged. She wondered, fearfully, who Rose Pledger had been.

Thoughts like that didn't seem to bother Allie. Allie had other thoughts. The two of them went back to the hotel. There wasn't anywhere else for them to go. They didn't dare spend any money until they made some.

Allie made right for her own room. Something was eating her. She didn't want to see anybody. So Janey was left alone and fell into an uneasy sleep. Perhaps it was the bus trip or the night before but she was tired out.

When she woke up everything felt different. It was night. It was the kind of exciting summer night, dreamy and sultry, when anything might happen. But Janey didn't want anything to happen. She wanted to stay where she was.

Allie wouldn't have it that way. Allie made her get up and get dressed. Allie was excited and all ready to go on the town, even if there was something funny at the back of her eyes that hadn't been there earlier.

Janey got dressed, and looked at the driving license before she tucked it into her purse. She still didn't want to be Rose Pledger. She didn't think Rose Pledger was very nice. But Allie was all for the Jickey Club, and the quickest buck she could make, and Purvis was waiting for them downstairs.

Allie called it a fast buck, but in her heart of hearts Janey knew Allie better than that. Allie just liked that kind of thing. She was ambitious, all right, but if she saw someone she liked, she went wild, and somehow the ambitions got lost somewhere along the way. She'd been like that even in High School. Sometimes it was Jim. Sometimes it was Bob. Now it was Purvis.

CHAPTER SIX

GOING BACK to the Jickey Club was almost like going home. Purvis made it that way. Every little man on the make has a place to relax, where he can feel he's arrived. And Purvis made himself agreeable. He had that 'the party's all on me' manner that good fakes always have. He didn't have his gang with him tonight, and that made him nicer. Or perhaps he was just breaking the girls in gradually. Who could say? Janey only knew she was grateful to have someone to hide behind.

It wasn't the first time Janey had been a third wheel. She was a natural born third wheel and knew it. But this time watching Allie work herself up made her uncomfortable. Instinctively she knew there was something wrong.

Purvis pushed open the double black glass doors to the bar, and posed there with them for a minute, until everybody who had swung round when the doors opened as people always do, had gotten an eyeful. He had an arm around each of them, like a production number from a Donald O'Connor movie. He caught the bartender's eye and winked.

The bartender shrugged, and made one of those furtive head movements towards the rear booth that seemed to be habit with him. Either he had a nervous tick or the heat was still on.

Janey could begin to spot the familiar faces now. She had plenty of time to do so. It wasn't so much that Allie and Purvis left her out, as that they never let her in. Allie was looking round the place.

"Where's that girl?" she asked.

"What girl?"

"You know. Vera. The stuck up one."

Purvis looked amused. "She's busy tonight."

"I'll bet."

"You'd lose it, she's visiting her folks."

"You know a lot about her," said Allie. Her eyes were hard and tense.

If Purvis was upset, he didn't show it. "She's one of the local characters, like me. She's really here a lot. She works out of here, if you get what I mean."

"What does she do, or am I wrong?"

"You're wrong," said Purvis. "She does this and that. I don't know. Who cares?" He took her hand and gave her a big wide grin, wriggling himself closer to her in the booth. "Look at Janey, Janey looks real prim."

They both looked at Janey. Allie was rapidly getting drunk. And Purvis was acting drunk, but he wasn't drunk. Outwardly he and Allie had been mauling each other for half an hour. But inside he was dead sober, dangerous, and positively cool. Janey was embarrassed. But Purvis had caught her eye. He had seen that she knew. It made him smile, and his slightly pointed, very white teeth showed for a moment between his soft red lips.

She didn't quite know what she knew. But she mistrusted him. She looked at Allie. But when she was excited Allie never noticed anything, and her body somehow got out of gear. She was pressed up close to Purvis, and he seemed to be enjoying it. Suddenly Janey wished she were somewhere else.

She looked round the bar, but no one was noticing her. It was a strange crowd, yet everybody seemed to look alike. They had the same bleached look, and the B-girls on their stools might just as well have been operating sewing machines, for all the passion they put into the act. Even the fat man was there. He, at least, was looking them over.

Allie wanted another drink. Purvis seemed to be making her uneasy. "What are you so fidgety about?" she demanded.

"I got to go on soon."

"Go on what?"

"I sing here, remember?"

"I thought that was free vaudeville, or something. Amateur night. Someone should have told you, Major Bowe's been dead a long time."

Purvis' eyes looked unpleasant. Then he decided to laugh it off. "I do all right," he said.

"Yeah. Let's see your scrapbooks!" said Allie. She hadn't meant to displease him, but now that she'd started, she had to go on with it. Maybe she hadn't learned how to hold her liquor yet.

Purvis got up and walked away. Allie looked startled. She sat very still. "I shouldn't have said that," she said solemnly.

Jane didn't say anything.

"What are you staring at me for? You think I've had too much or something?"

"He won't mind."

"You bet he won't. He knows when he's got something good. He's a real sweetie," said Allie. She giggled. "This can't be much fun for you. Why don't you go get some fun, Janey?"

"I'm all right."

Allie looked irritated. "You might be Grandma Moses or something. You've got a doctor to pay, remember?"

Janey shrank back against the booth, but before Allie could go on, Purvis was standing in front of them. His face was triumphantly flushed. "Here," he said, and handed over a big purple leather book. "Maybe that will convince you. I gotta go on now."

"He means it," said Allie. "A joint like this, and he calls it his art."

Purvis looked at her coolly, just looking her over, and she settled down. Then he turned on his heel and worked his way

through the crowd to the bandstand at the end of the room. He wasn't in the first number. The first number was just a teaser.

"Maybe he owns the place, or something," said Allie, still being scornful, but she pulled the scrapbook over to her and opened it.

"He means what he says," she said. "Come round and sit by me."

Janey did as she was told.

The book was full of clippings, and playbills, and old photographs. You could tell right off that Purvis had thought a lot of himself for quite a long time now. The pictures were there to prove it. Purvis was the glamour boy nobody likes who always manages to be Class President anyway, and nobody can figure out how it happened. Allie looked at all the pictures carefully. She would have been curious about any man, but about these pictures of Purvis she seemed doubly curious. It was as though she was shopping for him.

He had sung around here and there. The playbills proved that. Everything from amateur nights to small ratty clubs. He was determined about it.

Behind them came the sexy thwang of his guitar, and he began to cut loose. Allie had turned the page to a big publicity photograph, glossy and shiny. It was clearly the prize of the collection. A chrome mike leered out of the right hand corner of the picture. Behind it a man in a black shirt, a beige tie, and glasses disappeared into a cello. And right out there, filling the whole picture, was Purvis. It was quite a picture. It was in color, and he had that poached blue look people always have in color, when it is underexposed.

When he sang he stomped and jittered up and down and threw himself around, with his eyes closed, and he had the hips for it. It was as though his body were swung from steel ball bearings instead of a pelvis. He wore white pants with a thin belt around a slim waist, and an oatmeal sportcoat. His guitar was cradled like a woman in a convertible, and he was plucking away at it in a sort of dreamy ecstasy. His mouth was wide open, his eyes were shut, he was clearly yelling his head off, and he looked as though singing hurt him so much it was just wonderful.

Behind her Purvis' voice mumbled and shook. He was tearing his way through something called *Hungover Heart*. Allie looked at the picture.

"He's wonderful," she said. "He's just wonderful. He's got style."

Nobody in that bar was going to get carried away, if he could help it, but Purvis was in good form. He'd just made a new killing, maybe. He put his voice into it, and carried them with him. He sounded different. There were catcalls and whistles, but he just went right on. Allie's eyes were glazed with excitement. She jumped up, past Janey, and stood on the floor. Maybe she didn't know what she was doing.

"Oh spit on me, Purvis," she shouted. "Spit on me." Probably he didn't even hear her, but the crowd did. It caught them. Maybe she was right. For a minute there Purvis was really somebody.

It was more than Janey could take. She felt something drawing her into this world, that she wanted to resist, and knew she couldn't. She looked across the floor, and caught the eye of someone leaning out of a booth. She couldn't know how pretty she looked when she was flushed. She couldn't know it was Torrey, either, sitting there with Sanducci. But she did know sure as shooting that he was going to get up and come over to her. She wanted that and yet she knew she didn't want it. She glanced at Allie, but Allie wasn't going to be any help. She turned and ran out of the club. She just couldn't help it.

She went back to the hotel, through the sexy streets. But she didn't know they were sexy yet. She didn't have her eyes opened. She was so tight that she didn't know whether she fainted or fell asleep, but when she woke up, she still had her clothes on. Something had woke her up. It took her a moment to hear what.

The sounds came from Allie's room. They were instantly recognizable. Janey had been brought up by a sour old aunt, but everybody knows those furtive night noises, like mice scurrying through leaves. Everybody knows what is going on. Somebody is getting it, and getting it good. It was horrible. Janey remembered that quick look at the sound film, before it played through. After all, it was Allie in there, but an Allie gone wild. And all over the hotel people must be making sounds like that, all but her.

It was useless to pretend she was somewhere else or to go back to sleep. She heard the heavy rustle of springs. And Allie didn't care what she said. Where did she get words like that? Janey had never heard her use them before.

Once Janey had come out of Church and seen a couple of big black hounds hung up beside the walk, and nobody did anything about it, but just pretended they weren't there. But they had been there, and Janey had seen them.

She knew who it was, of course. She just knew.

After a long time the moaning suddenly stopped. Janey bit her pillow. It was almost over. She waited for the sounds of someone leaving. But they didn't come. She waited and waited, but they didn't come. Then she heard soft murmurs. Then she fell asleep again, shuddering, and heard nothing.

Next morning, when she went into Allie's room first thing, Allie was alone in bed, sitting up with a newspaper and her compact, doing things to herself, and looking sort of pleased. She didn't explain anything. And maybe she was a little anxious.

"How did you make out?" she asked.

Janey shrugged, wide—eyed. "I—I went to bed."

Allie didn't seem displeased. "You would," she said. "The trouble with us is, we're dull. Get dressed and we'll go shopping."

"Can we afford to?"

Allie hesitated and bit her lip. "You bet we can," she said. "Besides, nice clothes are business expenses." She peered into her mirror. "You know," she said, sort of wondering, "I'm pretty. I'm just really pretty." There was a new hardness in the slack of her babyish jaw as she said it. "You know, I bet I could be anybody I want."

"Of course you could."

Allie looked up at her sidewise. "Maybe now I don't want to," she said. She snuggled down into the bed with a contented sigh. But her face was still a little anxious. "Aren't you glad now we came?"

"I am if you are."

Allie frowned and cocked her head on one side. "The next thing to do is to do something about you," she said. "I'll ask Purvis. He can fix you up."

Janey's nightgown caught on the foot of the bed. "Well, go on, get ready," said Allie impatiently. Janey did as she was told.

Then they went shopping. It was just paradise. Manteca didn't have any stores like these. Janey had never been in stores like that in her life before. Neither had Allie, but Allie acted as though she had. Not that they bought much, but they felt as though they could, and that made all the difference. Allie was feeling so good she even bought Janey a purse, a big leather cylinder studded with brass nailheads, to wear by a strap over one arm.

"Where did you get all that money?" asked Janey, after they came out of the white marble store, into Union Square, one of the smarter sections of town.

"That's not money, that's bait," said Allie. She blinked at the Square. "We won't be in the Tenderloin long. I like it better up here."

Janey did too, but she'd never have dared say so. As long as Allie left her alone, she was almost content, except for one thing.

"How are we going to find a man?" she asked.

"What man?"

"You know what I mean. To see about me."

"You'll keep for a few days," said Allie. She patted Janey fondly. "With money," she said. "You wait and see. Your break will come next. I'll lend you a dress or something."

Janey knew it was useless to say anything else. Allie couldn't stop for anything when she got in a good mood like this. And she couldn't bring herself to ask Purvis, even though during the next three days she saw a lot of him.

Every night they went to the Jickey Club. Every night they sat in the booth and Purvis sang. But he was getting impatient.

"Why don't you wise up?" he'd ask her. She didn't have any answer to that. And the man at the bar still had his eye on her. She'd just go back to the hotel, and every night she'd lie awake, listening to those same noises. Except now Purvis left at about four in the morning or so. He said he had things to do. He was getting impatient.

It never even occurred to Allie that he was just softening her up. It didn't occur to Janey either. But she knew something was wrong.

Something was wrong with Allie, too. Vera still wasn't around. And she couldn't really enjoy herself, unless she could sort of show off before Vera. Somehow she just seemed to know that Vera meant more to Purvis then she did.

By Thursday things had fallen into a routine. The girls would go down to the Jickey at about nine-thirty and take a booth. Purvis would show up at ten. Then he would go back with Allie, except now sometimes he couldn't make it. Allie didn't like that. But he was generous enough. He paid for all the drinks.

"Where does he get it from?" asked Janey, vaguely disturbed.

"Who cares? He's got it, hasn't he, and he spends it," said Allie. The subject didn't seem to interest her. She was watching the door. And Thursday would be the night Vera showed up again just as Purvis came in behind her. She reached out one of her thin, transparent hands and stopped him.

Purvis looked worried. He took her arm and led her over towards the booth, talking rapidly. Vera was laughing. But her dark little eyes snapped and popped scornfully. She was really giving him the business about something. Purvis only shrugged.

When he went to sing, the three girls were left alone. They were silent for a while. That didn't prevent Allie from parading in front of Vera.

It didn't work.

Vera was funny. She smelled bad, like rubber when it gets too hot. Indeed there was something rubbery about her. She was all the wrong ages, like a doll. She had the same movements. Perhaps that was what made her look Chinese. But there was something veiled and ruthless in her eyes, too, that made her anything but nice. Yet she was small boned and very beautiful. It was rather that beauty didn't seem to matter to her at all, except in a knowing, professional way. She looked as though she were after something else, and Janey didn't like the way she looked at her.

Allie and Vera hated each other at sight. Janey waited for the explosion. But there wasn't any explosion. No matter what Allie did, Vera only seemed amused and superior. Which of course made Allie all the angrier.

Purvis finished his numbers and came back towards the table. Allie was real sweet to him. She wanted him to cuddle right up to her.

"I can't honey," he said. His eyes flickered over the three of them. "I got business."

"Real business?" asked Vera. Her voice was unexpectedly throaty, but for the first time she seemed tense.

He smiled at her. With him a smile could be a glare. Then he nodded.

"With Pedersen?"

"Yes."

"Well, take care of yourself." Vera slid expertly out of the booth. Allie got up to follow.

"I told you to stay here," snapped Purvis.

Allie pouted.

Vera had had enough of them. "Tell her to tell her little friend it's about time she hustled for her keep," she said and sauntered off to the bar. She sat down there without turning around.

Janey looked scared, and Purvis laughed. "Yeah," he said. "You know, it's an idea at that." He paused. "I'm sorry, kid, but I really got things to do. I'll see you later." Allie seemed to make him uncomfortable.

Allie looked vengeful. She breathed heavily.

"One thing," said Purvis. "You know how it is. You get a friend, I get a cut." He saw she didn't understand. He seemed to relent. "I'll come round to the hotel later."

"Promise," said Allie.

"Sure I promise," he said easily. He turned and loped for the door. Allie sat there until he had gone, drumming her fingers against the table top. Vera turned round and peered at them with a snotty expression on her face. Allie started to get up. Janey followed her.

"No," said Allie. "You leave me alone. He's right. You've got to start earning your keep sometime."

"Not now."

"I don't want you along," shouted Allie. As far as she was concerned she had been shown up for a sucker, and in front of Vera, too. She was on the edge of tears. She shoved Janey back into her seat and then rushed out of the place.

Janey was alone. She was so embarrassed she didn't even see where she was for half an hour. But she knew Allie meant it. She just felt it in her bones that Allie was getting ready to cast her off. There wasn't anything else she could do but hustle. She couldn't sit alone in the booth the rest of the night, and she didn't dare go back to the hotel with Allie in this mood. She looked around her uncertainly, and saw that the fat salesman type who haunted the place was looking her over. She tried not to catch his eye, but he was so persistent and so clever at it, that she knew eventually she would. And then, whether she smiled or not, he'd come galloping over. She just knew what that moustache of his would feel like, and he had a sticky come-on smile that was like flypaper.

Just as the salesmen looked as though he might be getting somewhere, and she didn't have anywhere to look but at him, the door opened, and the two men she now knew were plainclothesmen came in, and the nice one caught her eye. She recognized him now. He was the man who had stared at them at the station. His glance was just beginning to slide over her, when out of sheer desperation she smiled at him.

He looked round, saw the salesman, took in the situation, and instead of working his way through the room, dawdled by the door. The salesman turned round on his stool and ordered another drink. The plainclothesman, it was Torrey, raised his hand and made a circle with his thumb and forefinger, grinning at her.

Suddenly she liked him and felt warm inside. She wished desperately he would come over. But he didn't. Perhaps that was because of Sanducci, the guy he was with. She didn't want to order another drink, either. She sat there very tightly, feeling the hard, rough wood of the bench seat against her buttocks, and tried to pretend she was somewhere else again.

But all the time she wanted to speak to him. And it wasn't so much that she wanted too, as she just couldn't help it.

He made a movement towards the booth, and Sanducci hauled him back.

"Where do you think you're going?"

"Nowhere. I thought I'd check her papers. She looks kind of young."

"Any checking that gets done round here, I do. Hell, you could upset the whole works. Do I make myself clear?" Sanducci winked at Vera.

"You make yourself clear."

"You want to speak to a chick, then say so, that's your business. Checking is mine."

"Why should I want to speak to her?" Torrey looked at Sanducci warily.

"I've got eyes," said Sanducci. He shrugged his shoulders. "Go on. I won't tell no tales."

Torrey wasn't so sure. But even then he might have gone over, if Vera hadn't caught what was going on. She turned on her stool and watched Janey attentively, in a new way, and Janey couldn't take much of that. She felt self-conscious enough already.

The whole setup was ridiculous. A moment ago the room had been crowded. Now there was just the four of them alone in it, all looking each other over. Janey could feel herself blush.

Even then it might have worked out, but Sanducci turned round on Torrey. "How about it, boy?" he asked. "Is it a deal? Anything you want to do with her, I won't see it. She looks adaptable, if you like 'em that young."

That wasn't Torrey's approach to women. And no matter what was going on, he didn't think Janey was that kind of woman either. He was embarrassed for her. He didn't know what to do. He shrugged the thing off, even while he watched her.

Janey had heard Sanducci. Keeping her eyes down and her tears back, she sidled out of the room towards the door. She could feel Vera's eyes boring into her back. She knew what Vera was probably saying. No doubt Sanducci was having a big laugh, too, and Torrey would know what she was. She went out the door, faced the cold, half empty street, and almost ran to *The Florida*.

As usual the desk clerk didn't seem surprised at anything. She slowed down and went up in the elevator. There was a light under Allie's door. Allie was waiting for Purvis. Janey could hear her pacing up and down inside the room. It took her a long time to get undressed and longer to get to sleep, but the light didn't go out and the pacing didn't stop. Janey shivered. When she got herself worked up, Allie would do anything. But there wasn't anything to do about it. She fell asleep at last.

And Purvis didn't come.

CHAPTER SEVEN

IT just drove Allie wild. Janey didn't go into her room, but she could hear her, and she kept out of her way. If Purvis thought that staying away would soften Allie up, Janey could have told him he was wrong. Very few people had ever dared to stand Allie up, but when they did, she went off her head. She never forgave them and she always got even. It was no time for something like that to happen. All Janey could do was to stay out of her way and hope for the best.

She sat on the bed in her own room and turned out her purse. Things were getting tough. She knew what she had come for, and every day's delay made matters that much worse. She stared blankly at her change. She had maybe five or six dollars and some small change. It was Allie who had the money, and even Allie had only had about fifty bucks when they arrived in town. It wouldn't last much longer.

Janey knew what that meant. She shuddered.

Sewn up into the lining of her purse was a soft little wad. It didn't add up to more than twenty dollars, but it was the only secret she had ever kept from Allie, or ever been able to keep. It was the only security she had, and she felt it with her fingers. If the worst came to the worst, it would pay her fare back to Manteca, except that there was nothing to go back to Manteca for. Certainly her aunt wouldn't help her, and if her aunt wouldn't, nobody else would. If she didn't do exactly as Allie told her to, in a few months she'd really be cooked. And yet somehow she couldn't bring herself to do what Allie did. And now there was Purvis to worry about.

In the next room Allie began to beat the top of the bureau with her fists.

Janey couldn't stand it any longer. She snatched up her purse and fled down the hall to the stairs. On the way out through the lobby the desk clerk tried to stop her. She knew what he wanted. She blushed with shame, but she just couldn't listen to him now. She went outside. She wanted to get away from that whole grimy district just as fast as she could.

Eventually she hit the smart section of the city, around Union Square. She had been walking briskly, as though she had somewhere to go or someone to meet. Now she slowed down, knowing she had no one. She found herself aimlessly following two girls off to meet their boyfriends at the St. Francis hotel. They were crisp, well brought-up girls, and clearly they knew exactly what to do in a big town. They'd been to all the right schools, and dancing class, and they were always asked to parties, and maybe even to the yearly coming out ball. She envied the way they pulled on their gloves. Back in Manteca none of the girls ever wore gloves. They met their boyfriends on the front steps of the hotel. Their boyfriends were slim, crew-cut, blonde, a little scared, and very grown up. They were everything boyfriends should be. They were innocent and they had money.

Janey watched them go into the hotel and then she walked on up the block, almost as though she were meeting somebody herself. She even knew who. It was that nice man in the bar, the one who had wanted to talk to her, only she didn't dare. He was different from the others. He wasn't the sort of man Allie approved of at all. But she sort of knew what his voice would be like without ever having heard it. His voice would be warm and kind and cheerful. And he had blue eyes in a tanned face. If he was here anywhere she'd have recognized him even across the square.

Of course he wasn't. It was only a private 'let's pretend' game. If he had been there, she wouldn't have dared to speak to him anyway.

Suddenly the bright, smart square didn't cheer her up any more. She passed the shops, and felt the twenty dollars sewn in her purse, but she didn't dare spend it. Suddenly she felt shut out. All these people stared through her as though she wasn't even there, and at least in Manteca when you said good morning to strangers, they said good morning to you. Here you wouldn't dare say good morning to anybody, unless you worked in a shop or something.

She caught sight of herself in a shop window and stuck her tongue out, she looked so depressed. She hadn't any right to be depressed. She'd brought all this on herself, and Allie had offered to help her in the only way either of them could think of. It wasn't right for her to dodge Allie just because Allie was in one of her moods. She turned back towards the Tenderloin and went into the lobby of their hotel.

She'd forgotten all about the desk clerk. He hadn't forgotten about her. Even if he wasn't much more than thirty-five, he was still an unpleasant old man. He was the sort of man who just has to look at you to make you feel worse than you are.

He didn't have to say anything, so he didn't. He just lowered his comic book, shifted his gum, glanced at the pigeonholes behind him, and watched her.

Despite herself she stopped. She didn't want to speak to him now. She didn't have to. He looked her up and down slowly, as though wondering how much she could make if she got out and hustled right away.

Janey felt herself stiffen. She also felt herself blush. The lobby seemed very big. She smiled at him uncertainly. He didn't smile back. He did wink. She walked firmly to the elevator, and stood with her back to him. It seemed to her that the elevator would never come down.

He cleared his throat. "It's out of order," he said.

She half turned round.

"If folks don't pay their bills, we can't get it fixed," he told her. "Not that you'd know anything like that, now would you."

She fled up the stairs.

There was no sound from Allie's room, and no sign of any light under the door, though by this time in the afternoon the rooms were almost dark. Janey opened the door without knocking and went inside.

The shades were down. There was a creak from the bed. Allie was lying on her back, staring up at the ceiling, with her fists clenched at her sides. She'd had a tantrum. The handkerchief on the bed was limp with tears. She didn't speak.

Janey didn't know how to begin. "The desk clerk wants his rent," she said. "I don't like the way he looks at me."

"You may have to like it," said Allie. "We're broke." She went on staring at the ceiling.

Janey didn't say anything.

"Purvis was for free, you understand?" Allie propped herself up on one elbow. "He didn't give me a thing. Not a thing. You know what he is? He's a singing moron. That's all he cares about. I was just wild about him. I still am wild about him. He's just wonderful. Do you think I like waiting round in this crumby room all night long? Am I supposed to? Nobody stands me up, I don't care who he is.

"Maybe something came up," said Janey uncomfortably.

"Yeah. That Vera."

"Who's Vera?"

"That girl at the club. She has her hooks in him. Well, what's wrong with me? He liked me all right until she barged in. Am I ugly or something?"

She certainly looked ugly when she was mad. Janey picked up a pair of Allie's stockings off the floor and nervously rolled them up. They were snagged already. Allie never was very careful with her clothes. She always acted as though she only had to wear them once.

Janey looked at her round-eyed. "Is he your lover?" she asked. Somehow the question made her feel futile.

"Lover," said Allie. "What do you think I am? He isn't anything." She jumped up off the bed, and began to pace round the room. "I'll show him. He must think I'm some small-town hick or something. Probably he's having a big laugh over me with those dumb friends of his, right now. Why did he do that to me? Why?"

"He didn't do anything to you."

"He stood me up," shouted Allie. "Nobody stands me up. Nobody. And nobody's going to start now."

"He sort of runs that club. You'd better be careful."

"Do you think I'm afraid of anybody?" asked Allie. She stretched up her arms, and the armpits were raw where she had shaved them. Her little breasts jumped up and down with rage.

"No ..." said Janey slowly.

"I know what I'm going to do," said Allie. "The sooner we get back on the track the better off we'll be."

"What are you going to do?"

"Just you wait and see," said Allie. There was a malicious glint at the back of her eyes. "Anyone would think he had me shut up or something." Once Allie had an audience Allie began to pick up steam. Sometimes Janey thought that was the only reason Allie was her friend. She made a good audience.

Abruptly she sat down on the bed. "What about me?" she asked, and stared miserably at the linoleum pattern on the floor. It was the same as in her room.

Allie blinked at her. "Who cares about you?" she demanded. Her eyes were blind with anger. "It's probably too late now anyhow. So you have a baby? So what? Other people have babies. You can farm it out, can't you? It'll give you something to work for."

Janey stared at her with disbelief. Now it was out in the open, what was wrong with her. She thought it was horrible. She hadn't thought of it as a baby before. She'd just thought of it as something that was terribly wrong with her. It made her feel unclean. It wasn't her baby. It was something that man had done to her and then laughed about. She didn't even want to think about that man.

Somehow the pattern on the linoleum grew worse.

"But you said you'd help me," she said miserably.

"Go help yourself," said Allie shortly. "What do you expect me to do? Get out and leave me alone."

Allie had spoken to her like that before. Eventually Allie said something like that to everyone. But before Janey had always been able to go home until Allie got over it. Now all she could do was to go to the next room, and it wasn't even paid for.

She stayed in her own room all afternoon, chiefly because she was too depressed to leave it. At about nine she heard Allie's door slam and her footsteps down the corridor. They didn't come back, so Allie hadn't just gone to dinner. She knew where Allie had gone, and that made her wince. It meant trouble, and when Allie got in trouble someone always had to get her out of it. She got up and began to dress.

She was just struggling into her slip when there was a knock at the door. She thought it was Allie. She was filled with relief. She said "come in."

It wasn't Allie. She got the slip over her head, pulled it down, and saw it was the night clerk who was also the night manager. He leaned in the doorway and looked her up and down again. The only difference was that this time he didn't have his comic book.

He made her blush. Furiously she reached for her dress. She couldn't think of anything to say to him. It turned out she didn't get the chance.

"I sort of figured you girls weren't doing so well," he said. "I came about the rent."

"You'll get it."

He just sniffed and leaned against the wall. "Sure," he said. "Go on dressing. I like to watch people dress."

Janey didn't have any answer to that. The dress was all wrong, a wool dress with buttons down the front, but she wanted to get covered up as soon as possible. She stepped into it and began to do up the buttons.

He began to laugh. "You're sort of new at all this, aren't you," he said.

"New at what?"

"Oh you know what I mean all right." He leered and moved towards her. She closed her eyes. Suddenly he had his hands on her wrists. "Don't put it on," he said. "You'll just have to take it off again. Maybe the rent could wait."

He had halitosis and shovel teeth. She pulled herself away.

He was still pretending to be amused. "Okay," he said. "Okay, but it's no way to run a business."

She was blind with tears, not only because she didn't like him, but because she'd never be able to do what Allie wanted her to do. She reached into her purse, ripped out the lining, and shoved three of the five dollar bills at him. That left her a five.

He took the money and smoothed it out. "Well, that's another three days for the pair of you," he said. "I'm patient. I can wait. But what are you going to do then?"

"I don't know," she said. "Go away."

When he had gone, she looked bleakly at her purse. It was empty now, her safety money was gone, and she knew what that meant. It meant she was at Allie's mercy.

And mercy was something Allie didn't have much of.

She left the room, locked the door, and went to the Jickey Club.

CHAPTER EIGHT

A LLIE had gotten there an hour before. And no matter what Janey or anybody else might think, Allie felt just plumb scared to the pit of her stomach. Getting even with Purvis was one thing. She'd do that all right. But the way she had to do it made her feel sick just to think about.

Because she was an amateur. Before she'd always gone with men just for kicks. She was beginning to see that doing it for a living was somehow different. Somehow the kicks weren't there the way they should be. It was too much like work.

She was pretty early. She hoped she was there before Vera or Purvis or any of the regular gang who could crimp her style, and she was in luck. She was. She sidled up to the end of the bar, real grown-up, and ordered a scotch and water that wasn't as strong as it should have been. She tried to look casual while she cased the room.

Allie looked old for her age, real grown-up, and she'd had loads of adventures, more than she'd ever told Janey about. They hadn't happened quite the way she usually told them, either. Any girl who has to work as a waitress at fifteen learns a lot. A little town like Manteca isn't much, but salesmen and travelers are always going through, and they seem to think their license plates are invisible or something. They didn't care how young anybody was. Sometimes Allie wondered how people made out before the hydromatic shift was invented and the brake was rooted in the floor. It was uncomfortable enough as it was, and by the time she was sixteen she knew motels didn't necessarily make their living off families of five. She couldn't stay out all night, and that was okay with the motel people. They just rented the room again.

But this was different. She'd never even been inside a real bar before the Jickey Club, let alone earn her keep there. Usually people had just naturally given her things, except for the guys at the High School, who seemed to feel a drive in the folks' convertible was enough. But working as a waitress she'd learned one thing. When you weren't thinking of anything in particular, you met wonderful people. But when you needed a lift, you got stuck with the creeps. She didn't know where the handsome people were. Sometimes it seemed as though handsome people never went out at all. There wasn't a man in the bar under thirty-five or six.

It was all very well to pretend in front of Janey, but she never did anything brave unless she had a friend along as an audience. She just sat there, feeling wretched, and trying not to look it, until the liquor warmed her, and she felt less self-conscious.

At last she knew someone was staring at her, and looked up. The bar was always smoky and Allie was a little short-sighted. He was a short, enormously fat man with marble eyes and sleek sweaty skin, but at least he was there. The sight of him made her feet ache. She twitched her toes and gave him a great big, special smile, full of reserve, breeding, and the hint that perhaps he might have a chance. But there was something queer about him, she could sense that. She didn't like the look of him at all. On the other hand she couldn't still be there when Purvis turned up, either.

He went on staring at her until she could scream. There was something familiar about him she couldn't quite place. She wished he'd get a move on. She certainly wasn't going to make the next move towards him.

When she looked up from her drink again he was hovering near her. "Hi," she said. It was easy, really. It always was easy. Perhaps her voice sounded too girlish, but apart from that she thought she was all right. After all, the Jickey Club wasn't a soda fountain.

"Let's go sit in a booth," he said.

His voice was somehow stern. She recognized him now. He was Sanducci, one of those plain clothes dicks who drifted through the place. She was worried. But she gave him a tight little smile and walked ahead of him to the booth, holding her thighs very close together. She wondered if it was a pinch.

But Sanducci slid into the booth and began to be real affable. It didn't suit him. But at least it didn't mean a pinch. Allie looked him over, and went into her charming little girl from hunger routine. He seemed to take it well.

She relaxed and began to giggle, with one eye on the clock.

She wondered what he really wanted, or how much of it, and she wished he'd get round to the point. Purvis would be showing up soon. She couldn't have chosen better, even if Sanducci was repulsive. Purvis would see her with him and think she was turning informer, so the joint could be raided. Purvis might not remember it, but he'd told her a few things. If she mentioned that, he'd come round soon enough.

"Where's your friend?" she asked, and put her purse in her lap, so he'd keep his hands to himself for a while.

"Goofing off somewhere," said Sanducci. "Who cares about him?"

"Doesn't he check up on you?"

"I check up on him," said Sanducci. He glanced down at the purse. "You know a trick or two, don't you?"

Allie felt warm and flattered. She forgot her worries. She even forgot that she didn't like Sanducci much. At least everyone could see she had a man. She wondered what he'd pay, and it never even occurred to her he was pumping her. He'd given her a lot to drink and she wasn't used to drink. It made her giggle.

Sanducci saw Janey come in the door and went right on talking. In some ways Allie was a little hard to sum up.

Janey paused at the edge of the crowd, ignoring the few whistles the loiterers at the door gave her. Then she spotted Allie.

Sanducci watched her make up her mind. Then she came over to them. She didn't look very friendly.

That was because, if this was how Allie was going to get even with Purvis, Janey didn't want any part of it. Janey was scared of the police. She always had been, even as a little girl. Sanducci could smell it and he liked it. As far as he was concerned, that was one of the pleasures of being a policeman.

Allie looked up at her from a vast distance.

"You're the girl friend," said Sanducci. He had an oily smile. "Sit down. Sit down."

Janey sat. It seemed to her that she sat there forever. It certainly must have been a long time. When she looked up the atmosphere had somehow changed, and she knew there was going to be trouble.

Sanducci and Allie were cuddling on the opposite bench, and Allie had the giggles. Allie was sitting on the outside, but she wasn't making any effort to get away, probably because Sanducci wasn't making any real effort to keep her. He was just enjoying himself in his own way, for his own reasons.

Suddenly Purvis was standing in front of them. He was scowling, and he was all dressed up. He looked real sharp. But he had his gang behind him, and they didn't look sharp at all. They'd obviously come along to see Purvis get tough.

"Get up," he ordered.

Allie squinted at him out of an adolescent alcoholic haze.

"Who is it?"

"You know damn well who it is. I said, get up."

Allie's eyes narrowed and she looked stubborn. "Mister, I don't know you from Adam. Who's going to make me?"

Purvis grabbed her by her waist and jerked her up out of the booth.

"Hey," she said. She was genuinely startled. "Don't you see who I'm with?"

"Sure I see. You and me are going to have a talk."

"See what he says," said Allie, glancing at Sanducci.

"He doesn't say anything," said Purvis. He looked over her shoulder at Sanducci. "Do you, friend?"

Sanducci stirred uneasily, but he didn't say anything. Purvis propped Allie up between the booths and stood in front of her, slouching from hip to hip and looking her over.

"You try anything with me, and I'll have you run in," said Allie. "I got friends now."

"Who? Sanducci?"

"He's a cop, isn't he? He's sitting with me, isn't he?"

Purvis got a big kick out of that. "My, my," he said. "The schoolgirl's revenge. I guess maybe you think you've got quite a catch there."

Janey sat in the shadow of the booth. She refused to catch Sanducci's eye. Suddenly Purvis turned to Sanducci.

"Scram," he said.

"Ah Purvis, can it," said Sanducci.

"Yeah. You know something tells me perhaps you had the same idea I had about somebody. Well, stay off, see? I saw her first."

Sanducci didn't say anything. But he looked fit to be tied.

"You hear me?"

"Yeah," said Sanducci, "I heard you."

Purvis turned to Allie. "You're so primitive, you thought maybe you could make me jealous and angry and all that." Purvis looked pleased. "With Sanducci, yet. Well, I've got news for you. I'm civilized. I don't mind at all."

He put his thumbs in his pockets and swayed back and forth on his heels. His little group moved in closer.

"Honey, don't you know what racket I'm in?" he asked. "Don't you really? You think I'd waste my time if you weren't hungry for it? You think I ain't got anything better to do? I'm a singer, see? I'm real professional. Only I ain't got the breaks yet, so I have to eat. You understand me?"

"I don't want anything to do with you," said Allie. She turned towards Sanducci.

But Sanducci was watching Purvis. Purvis was maybe getting a little out of hand.

"Baby, you don't have much choice," Purvis told her. He turned wheedling. "You like me, don't you? You sure said you did. You're real attached to me. Well, I'm attached to you, too, whether you like it or not. Only I get paid for it. Hell, you should be lucky even to be seen with me. I got contacts."

"Some contacts."

"There's just one little thing, that's all. Anything you get, you pay me half. That's because I'm generous. Most guys would just give you eating money. You aren't worth much more. Didn't you ever hear of a pimp?"

Allie just laughed at him. But the laugh didn't come off.

"Maybe you'd rather be roughed up a little. Your friend here would like you fine then."

"Do something," said Allie to Sanducci.

"Sanducci won't do anything," said Purvis. "He gets his cut like the rest of us."

Allie stared at him. She took it hard.

"Aw, come on. I'll come and see you sometimes," said Purvis. "You're real hot stuff."

Janey watched them.

"Who's going to make me?" asked Allie. "I don't owe you a thing."

"It isn't a matter of owing. It's a matter of taking. You don't give, me and the boys here might not like it. Take a look at the boys, honey. Take a real close look. Then maybe you might change your mind. You're pretty now. You might not stay pretty much longer."

"Try and get it," said Allie. "Just try. I don't need you."

"That isn't what you used to say. Shall I tell the boys what you used to say? You thought I was just the fastest thing on two skates."

"I don't need anybody," said Allie. "You shut up."

Purvis grinned. "Well boys, it was this way," he drawled.

Allie spat at him.

Purvis started. He jerked like a snake. Then he pulled out a handkerchief and wiped it up. "My, my," he said. "Anyone would think you had Mexican blood or something."

Slowly he drew his left hand out of his pocket, twisted the ring on it, and slapped her repeatedly across the face. The bruises rose fast. "That should give you a few days to think it over," he said. "You aren't going to hustle anybody looking like that."

Allie screamed. The ring had cut her cheek. She turned to Sanducci. "Don't let him get away with it," she shouted.

Sanducci didn't move.

"He isn't going to do anything, honey," said Purvis. He grabbed her purse, took out the hand mirror, and shoved it in front of her. "Here. Look at yourself. You look real cute."

Pedersen and his gang stirred behind him. They'd enjoyed it. Allie saw that they'd enjoyed it. She swept the mirror out of his hand and it broke on the floor.

"That'll bring you bad luck, honey," he said.

"I can get along without you."

"Try it. Just try it." He looked round the bar coolly. Everybody was watching, of course. He liked that. "What are you going to do, earn a dollar a night in some crib? How you gonna pay for things? Where are you gonna get clothes. Where are you gonna hustle? You don't know nobody but us, baby. And we can keep you out of here all right." He held out his arms mockingly. "Be a good girl. Come and work for Papa. He only wants half of the take. He's reasonable." He chuckled.

"And you said you loved me."

"Maybe I did. Hell, somebody had to break you in. You've got a hick technique, baby. You're hot, but you're a hick. Besides, it's just like I'm your agent, or something. And who ever got a job without an agent? Ask Sanducci here. He's a cop. He knows all about agents."

He was right. He could shut her right off. And Allie knew it. Tears began to flow down her cheeks, and she was still the worse for wear from all those drinks. Janey tried to make herself invisible. Allie made a funny kind of strangled noise and bit Purvis suddenly on both wrists.

He jumped, rubbed his wrists, and really let her have it, with a broad hard slap, right in the middle of the nose. Her nose began to bleed.

Sanducci slid in front of Purvis. "Hey, we don't want any ruckus," he said. "Somebody'd better get her out of here."

"You can see how loyal he is," said Purvis. He was absolutely beaming. "Go push her down a manhole, I don't care."

Sanducci took Allie's arm and shoved her towards the door.

"Maybe you shouldn't have done that," said Pedersen, rubbing Purvis' wrists, where Allie had bitten them.

Purvis shrugged. "Who cares? She'll come round or I will. What difference does it make." He grinned. "But she sure looked silly when I hit her. Back in Manteca I guess she thinks she's hot stuff. We'll let her cool off a little first, that's all. Then we handle her." He turned round to the booth and caught sight of Janey. "Hey, you too, mouse," he said, jerking his head towards the door. "Out."

Janey got up and got out, edging her way past the whole bunch of them, while they made mock whistles and grinned at her.

Sanducci and Allie were ahead of her. She started after them, not even noticing the man who had followed her out of the bar. It was the fat salesman type who never seemed to get anywhere, the one with the rat eyes and the moustache. He pattered along behind her, making no effort to catch up. But he was following them all right.

Out in the air Allie didn't look so bad. Her face was beginning to swell and mottle. She looked as though she'd been pistol whipped. She was roaring mad, but she was trying to be seductive again. It wasn't getting her very far.

Sanducci looked at Janey with relief. "Here's your friend," he said. "She can get you home."

Allie looked surprised. "Aren't you coming up?"

He didn't even bother to answer.

Allie's nerves cracked, and she began to shriek at him. "Then why all the build up?" she demanded. "What's the matter, you queer or something?"

Her voice carried. Sanducci looked anxiously up and down the street. He was jiggling with impatience. "Nobody wants you now," he said. "Who cares."

Allie began to curse at the top of her lungs. Janey shivered.

"Yeah, what are you going to do about it?" demanded Sanducci. "Any time I feel like it, I run you in. And if you said anything about it, those pals of yours would cut you up into little pieces." They had reached an alley, and he turned rapidly and scuttled down it.

Behind them the fat man drew into a doorway, and looked at a display of orthopedic trusses and hernia belts. He didn't want to be seen either. But he followed them eagerly all the same.

Allie looked bewildered.

So was Janey, but she knew she had to get Allie off the streets fast. A block ahead of them the lights of the all night coffee joint streamed into the wet fog. The street was deserted, but she had no way of knowing how long it would be. She gave Allie enough time to repair the worst damage to her face out of her compact, which wasn't easy without a mirror. Then, taking her arm, she steered her towards the cafe. Allie was shivering now.

Behind them the fat man fell into step.

CHAPTER NINE

PLACES in the Tenderloin that stay open all night get used to anything. The clerk at the corner drugstore, for instance. One man wants a bottle of Cuprex for crabs. A girl comes in and buys two candy bars and a diaphragm inserter. It won't fit in her purse, she slips it into her stocking. Max Factor is good for bruises, but makes you look as though you'd fallen asleep at a cinemascope in technicolor. It's an education.

People who work in all night cafes are also immune to shock. Bob and Anna were immune to everything. In their line of work they had to be. A drunk they could handle most of the time, but it made them wary, and they kept a gun in the till. They paid a lot for protection, but one night they might get raided by accident. That could be awkward. Apart from that nothing bothered them much. When Allie and Janey came in, they didn't even look up. When the fat man came in right behind them, they did. His little habits weren't exactly unknown to them, but he paid cash, so it wasn't any of their affair. They naturally thought he'd come to ask them to fix him up. Bob had his telephone list right there handy. But the girls complained. They'd have to raise the rates on him, soon.

Some of the fog had come in the door with the fat man, and it revived five years' worth of old cooking smells, not that the smell in there wasn't bad enough at any time. About fifty thousand dead prawns had gone to a better world and left their stench behind them. The cooking fat was mixed with gunk. The only person who could have cleaned the coffee urns was a chimney sweep. But Bob and Anna didn't care. They went on serving their meals anyway, just as though it was real food.

Anna was the shifty one. She was only in her twenties, but she already had a heavy, sullen, slit-eyed Polish face. She was a one woman ghetto all by herself, but she could be kind when it suited her.

Allie was the kind of girl Anna wouldn't handle on a bet. She knew that kind. They were nothing but trouble. They wouldn't play ball. The other girl was a type that was hard at first, but easy afterwards. The only trouble you had with that type was easing it off when it got too old, and getting it on the circuit in the first place.

But business had been slow that night, there had been nobody to talk to, and the girls were the only people in the joint, unless you counted the fat man, Sparkman. Anna never liked to talk to Sparkman. He made her flesh creep. She went over to the girls.

"Honey, someone really worked you over," she said. "You should put some ice on that. What'll it be?"

"Hot chocolate," said Janey. Allie looked sullen.

"It doesn't do to get too smart too fast round here," said Anna chattily. "You girls from out of town?"

"Yes," said Janey. Poor thing thought Anna, she looked scared blue, but if they didn't want to talk, they didn't want to talk. She went off to make the chocolate, and through the service hatch, she could watch Sparkman moving up on them.

He didn't waste any time. It was funny, he never beat them up himself. He just liked to look at them when they had been. His moustache was quivering with excitement. Anna looked away.

Sparkman looked the girls over, and pretended Anna wasn't even there. Sparkman was forty-five, sold plumbing, and had a wife and two kids out in the Sunset District somewhere. It was his second wife. The kids were hers. He was very fond of them. He was a good salesman. He had a weak heart, a varicose vein in his left leg, his wife never asked any questions, and he lived in terror of being blackmailed. He'd been forced to augment his income occasionally himself, and he knew how it was done. Not that he had ever really blackmailed anybody, but he was a member of the Sheriff's Posse and the initiation fee was high. He was the one who could always get hold of hot movies for smokers. In a locked closet at home he had a stack of eight by ten glossy photographs a foot high. He looked at them sometimes, when his wife was away and the kids were in bed. He had a passion for pictures of naked girls posed with ducks and white geese. He even had some color slides of that sort of thing, taken in Reno during his divorce. The best one he carried in the inner compartment of his wallet. That was the sort of thing he liked. Sometimes it came expensive.

Right now, though, he was all sympathy.

There was something furtive about Sparkman. Even if he had shouted his head off, he would still have seemed furtive. He glanced around him.

"I saw the beating you took back there," he said. "It was pretty bad." His voice dripped sympathy.

"Yeah," snapped Allie. "Did you enjoy it?"

That took Sparkman aback. Watching him from the kitchen serving window, Anna chuckled. She knew what he was up to, of course, but she was too interested to break it up. Allie looked like a tough one. She wanted to see what happened.

"It was just terrible," said Sparkman. He oozed sympathy. His hobby was befriending fallen girls. The farther they'd fallen, the better he liked them. He had other little hobbies, too. "They're a tough crowd, in there. Someone should have told you that. I've seen you in there before."

"Mister, I saw you too," said Allie. She took a gulp of her chocolate, but she was beginning to look at him curiously. Clearly he wasn't the usual kind of middle aged salesman, and she was beginning to wonder what the difference was.

Sparkman's face clouded over. He didn't like to be watched, and they might be informers. You never knew who was working for the police these days. He looked towards the kitchen, and Anna gave him a frigid smile.

Janey watched helplessly. She knew the signs. Allie was beginning to take an interest. No doubt Sparkman was trying to be kind, but she found it difficult somehow to look him in the eye. He embarrassed her.

Sparkman quivered. Allie's bruises were still getting puffy. He reached out a hand.

"Hey, what are you doing?" Allie demanded. Automatically she flinched away.

"I just wanted to feel how bad they were."

Allie looked at him and then laughed uneasily. "They're bad enough."

"Maybe I could help. I mean one of my friends used to be a boxer. He got beat up bad. We used to have to patch him up." Sparkman shrugged. "You can't go back to the Jickey looking like that."

"That was the idea. Purvis is a real sweet boy."

"He's the one in the peg pants who sings," said Sparkman, frowning.

"He does other things, too."

Sparkman looked up quickly. "You know what he does?"

"Well, mister, you watched him," said Allie. Apparently it was the wrong thing to say. Sparkman sighed.

"What're you going to do now?" he asked. His voice skidded delicately away from some kind of danger zone of its own.

For some reason or other he reminded Janey of that basement they had gone down into to get their forged identity cards, and the hunched up man with his funny films. She squirmed.

"Get me some clothes, and a rest, and I'll really show that louse where he can go," snapped Allie.

"You got any money?"

"Enough," said Allie, and looked at him sideways. Anna came out of the kitchen and bustled over to them. They said they didn't want anything. Sparkman paid her for all three of them. She sniffed and waddled to the cash register. He watched her silently until she went back to the kitchen.

"I could maybe get you a couple of jobs. Just to tide you over. I know some people," said Sparkman.

"Yeah, I'll bet," said Allie.

Sparkman blushed. When he blushed he looked like a wicked baby. "They'd be kosher," he said.

"Of course."

"I mean it." He hesitated. "For both of you. You ever wait on table or anything like that?"

"Do I look like a waitress?" snapped Allie.

Sparkman shrugged. "Well, you come from a small town. You probably worked summers, or something."

"Mister, you know a hell of a lot about us, it seems to me."

Under Allie's left cheek, close to her nose, the worst bruise was turning yellow at the edges. Sparkman watched it. He felt tired. The heat in the restaurant was bringing the bruises up. "What have you got to lose?" he asked. "You need a nest egg, don't you?"

"Yeah, but I don't want to lay it," said Allie.

Sparkman chuckled, and took her arm. "Come on," he said. "I'll walk you back to your hotel."

Allie flinched, but she didn't make any effort to shake off his arm. They turned towards the door, and as they left, Anna came out of the kitchen and watched them leave. Two girls at once was a departure for Sparkman. In a way she admired him for it. She kept a cross file on her customers and their habits. This would be something to add to it.

Anna was wrong. Sparkman didn't have anything like that in mind at all. On the way back to the hotel, he gave them a pep talk about jobs. But he didn't give them a pep talk about anything else. Allie was puzzled. Nobody helped you for nothing, and he was pretty revolting, but you had to get money somewhere. She naturally thought he was going to come up with her, with Janey as a third wheel, as usual, unless maybe he had ideas. She'd heard about that sort of thing. She wondered what Janey would do about it, if he had.

But Sparkman wouldn't even come into the lobby. He peered into the lobby, over their heads, but he wouldn't go any farther than the entry way. In fact, it was clear the one thing he didn't want to do was to go upstairs with them. All round, it was a nothing doing evening, but Allie was too tired to feel mad.

"Mister," she said, "are you serious?"

"I'll give you a ring in the morning," he said.

"But why?"

Sparkman never quite understood why himself. He looked like a scared rabbit. Sometimes he thought there was a cop round every corner. He was a respectable businessman. He had to be careful.

Allie gave it up. "Well, if you mean it, it's damn nice of you," she said. She gave him a big smile that it hurt her to make, because of what Purvis had done to her. "You don't want to come up, really?"

He really didn't. He said good night and pattered down the street. He looked ready to cry. Allie looked after him, shrugged, and went into the hotel. The two girls didn't speak until they reached their own corridor.

"Well, what do you make of that?" asked Allie, fumbling for her key.

Janey shivered. "He gave me the creeps."

"He's creepy all right. But we could sure use those jobs. If they're real that is." She sighed, unlocked the door, and took off her pumps. The heels and toes of her stockings were sticky with sweat. "So far we haven't done so well, have we?" She gave Janey a wan smile.

"What do you suppose he wants?"

Allie laughed. "Whatever it is, he won't get it. He's had his chance, and boy was I tired. Anything he wants from now on in, he can just look at."

She stared at Janey for a minute. "Go to bed," she said. "You look awful. He won't phone. Tomorrow we'll have to figure out what to do."

Janey leaned against the door. "Can't I stay with you? I don't want to be alone."

"Neither do I," said Allie. "I don't know what we're going to do. Some character, he was."

They were so tired, they slept in their slips, without taking anything else off. Janey woke up at about three. Allie was crying in her sleep. They hugged each other, because they were scared. Only Allie wasn't awake enough to know it.

At nine the phone woke them up. Allie answered it. It was sort of hard to hear, because the desk clerk was listening in, and he had asthma. When she put the phone down she was frowning.

"Well imagine that," she said. "He meant it."

CHAPTER TEN

H E HAD GOTTEN them jobs, all right, but not together. Maybe he believed in dividing people up and letting them think it over. Maybe it just happened that way. Allie's was in a drive-in. The way she felt about it, the sooner she picked up some cash, the sooner she'd be able to quit. She knew she couldn't stick to it for more than a week, but she needed the cash. They both did.

Allie had some funny ideas. She didn't even live from day to day. She just lived right here and now. She must have had some idea of what she wanted when she came to San Francisco. But whatever it had been, she had forgotten about it, and she was here now. Of course something would have to be done about Janey. And one day, of course, she'd be well off and have a house with a swimming pool. She wanted nice clothes and a husband who was away a lot and very handsome. But that wasn't the same as being ambitious. She never claimed to be ambitious. She just wanted to have a good time.

So the drive-in didn't bother her much. She was all set to make the most of it. And to do that, she had to learn the ropes.

It didn't take her long. The drive-in was the toughest in the city, if that was what you were looking for. The crowd that went in during the evening hadn't heard about the crowd that came in from midnight until two. The police had.

At first the police gave her the creeps. Then she got used to them. She even tried to persuade herself that they were good joes. Maybe they had been once. Nonetheless she stayed away from them. It wasn't hard to do. She was working outside. They arrived in clumps of two or three on their patrol cycles, went inside, and hunched over the counter together. They were young and thin. They looked like dangerous beetles. They were sexy. She avoided them, but she couldn't take her eyes off them. She was getting interested in men again.

It was two days later, and though she didn't want to admit it, she knew she was hiding out. The bruises on her face she could cover up with blemish cream. But the other bruises hurt more. Purvis had made a fool of her and she'd never been so humiliated in her life. She could hardly wait to get even with him, she didn't care how.

She did well on tips, but by the third night she was bored, even though she hadn't missed a thing that was going on. Nobody seemed eager to pick her up. In joints like this they seldom were. She'd been a waitress before, and she knew the ropes. But she didn't like them.

A bunch of crazy kids always came in about midnight, sliding up in hot rods and sports cars that had come from nowhere in particular. They might whistle after her, but she didn't pay them much mind. Kids like that didn't have much cash, and what they did have all went in their cars. There wasn't apt to be much left over for her, and she wasn't exactly in this for free.

If things went on this way, she'd have to go back to Sparkman. She had to start somewhere. She wasn't going to get anywhere in a drive-in. A waitress wasn't even a call girl. A waitress was just a quick lay.

A car slid in beside her. She couldn't see a thing through the windshield, but she gave it a big eager smile and did her little sexual toddle out to the window. But she didn't feel cuddly and soft. She felt cold. The drive-in provided kid boots with tassels, short red satin shorts, a white blouse, and a bolero jacket. The weather was foggy, and she had gooseflesh. The boots didn't quite fit, and she had to be careful how she carried a tray.

It was Pedersen, Purvis' friend, and a bunch of his friends, pimply kids acting tough, mostly. That threw her off balance. It also scared her. She didn't look at their faces. She looked at their belts. They weren't wearing any. Instead they had chains held with padlocks. She wondered what that meant. It seemed right up Sparkman's alley.

"We aren't interested," the driver said. "We only want food, honey, on a plate."

Pedersen craned over from the back seat. He was wearing a dirty t-shirt and a visor cap. "Well, well, look who's here," he said. "And my don't you look pretty."

His voice was a big leer. Allie couldn't get away from them fast enough. But they wouldn't let her go. The driver grabbed her arm. "Say, you're cute," he said. "Who hit you?"

"Maybe she likes that sort of thing. Maybe she'd like some more," growled Pedersen. His voice was an imitation of Purvis'.

A car slid into one of her stations and its horn honked.

"I gotta go," said Allie. She was getting scared.

"She gotta go."

"It's round to the left honey," said the driver. "Don't you know the layout yet?"

"Oh let her go."

Allie fled, and minced round to the other car. But she didn't get relief there either. It was Sanducci. He rolled the window down and stared at her. He was in uniform tonight, even though it was a private car.

"I see you're getting on," he said. "You girls never learn, do you?"

"I wasn't doing anything."

"Looked as though you were hustling, to me."

"I work here. I can't help it if they talk to me."

"I'm not talking. I just watch."

"Yeah, I know."

Sanducci looked angry. "You shouldn't speak to me that way. It might not be wise."

"You want to order?"

"Hell, no," said Sanducci. "Sparkman get you this job?"

"What if he did?"

Sanducci shrugged. "You don't know much, do you? I feel real sorry for you." He nodded over towards the other car. "I see your friends found you okay."

"Some friends."

"They're real nice boys," said Sanducci. "They do real well."

Allie lost her head. "If you don't want to order, you can't park here."

Sanducci didn't like that either. He started the engine. "I'll be keeping an eye on you," he said. "I thought you might like to know." He put the car into reverse and roared out into the parking area, narrowly missing a white convertible. Allie went back to the other car, picking up their order on the way. She clamped it onto the window, not saying a thing.

"You've got friends," said the driver after a while.

"Some friends."

Allie didn't say anything.

"Close friends," said Pedersen. He lolled in the back seat, watching her. "I wouldn't go telling them anything. It might not be such a hot idea. Sanducci may be okay, but a cop's a cop."

"What would I tell them?"

"I dunno. What would she tell them?" asked Pedersen. The others just grinned.

They gave Allie the creeps. She liked to have nightmares while she was asleep. She told them so.

They just laughed. But they watched her. She knew they were watching her. She was scared. She was glad when they went away. She was badly rattled. And when she was rattled, she knew she might do anything. That was okay, but she didn't want to get caught at it, that was all.

She worked from nine until two-thirty. The rest of the evening nothing happened, except the fog got thicker and she got colder.

At two-fifteen business was slow. She ducked round the side of the drive-in, into the dead-end corridor that led to the rest rooms. She thought she might as well have a cigarette. The girls weren't allowed to smoke on duty, and at least the rest room was warm. She turned the corner and ran smack into somebody leaning against the wall.

It was Pedersen, and he was waiting for her. She turned to get out, but he grabbed her, and spun her round, so that she stood on the other side of him, while he blocked the exit.

"The boys thought maybe I should talk to you," he said.

"What do you want?"

He shrugged. He was thin and scrawny, and although he didn't look tough, he was tough. His t-shirt was torn. His jeans were filthy, and so were his boots. "What've you been telling Sanducci?" he asked.

"What's it to you?"

"Plenty. You wouldn't be a stool would you? We don't like stools."

Allie couldn't say anything. She was fascinated by his belt.

"Well?" he said. "Start talking."

She shook her head. She whimpered. He seemed to like that. He grinned and swaggered. "Come on," he said. "Purvis must've said something. He wouldn't like it to get round. We don't like girls getting chummy with Sanducci. He's a pill. The heat's on. He might get ideas."

Allie shook her head.

He unclasped the padlock, and snaked it out of his belt loops.

She ducked. With the clasp open, it made a dreadful weapon. It rattled through the air. Pedersen laughed, and gave a jump.

"Come on," he said. "Talk. You need what's left of that face. Come on." He had hit her legs. It stung. Now he aimed higher.

She sobbed and clawed for the lock. Somehow she caught it and tugged. He had been holding it loosely. It came away in her hand, and he lost balance. She was terrified. She lashed out again and again. The buckle on one of his boots had caught on something. It made him stumble. She hit with the chain. He bellowed. She hit again and again, and managed to get round him. She took off across the lot. She didn't care who saw her. She just had to get out of there. Apparently she hadn't hurt Pedersen badly. She heard him curse, and then he was pounding the pavement behind her.

She still had the chain in her hand. She half turned and flung it after him. He was passing under a street light. She'd gotten him right in the face, and he was streaming with blood. She heard a car start up. She panicked. After all, he'd have cronies round somewhere. Unless she got off the streets she didn't have a chance, and Pedersen would murder her. It was hard to run. She headed down the street.

Two cars swung in from the other end. One she recognized. It belonged to the gang. She half turned and saw Pedersen gaining on her. There were no police around. There never were when you needed them. She didn't scream. She only whimpered.

The other car put on a spurt and drew alongside her. The door opened. Someone told her to get in.

She didn't hesitate. She got in. The car took off.

It was Sparkman. She wasn't even surprised. "Oh my," he said. "Oh my." He had the giggles. He was delighted. "Oh my, you really gave it to him."

Allie didn't say anything.

The other car drew into the curb behind them, and took Pedersen aboard. Sparkman didn't have to worry about the police. Sparkman was respectable. But Pedersen had to get off the streets.

"Are they following?" asked Sparkman.

They went through an arterial. Allie looked back. The other car had turned left on two wheels. It didn't have a muffler. You could hear it going. There was another car behind them now, but that didn't mean anything. Allie slumped in her seat and said no.

Sparkman looked at her costume and the cut on her leg. "You travel with a fast crowd," he said. He switched on the radio.

"How come you were there?"

Sparkman didn't answer. He went on driving. He made Allie uneasy. She didn't think he was dangerous or anything, but he was certainly queer.

"I always wanted to get in with that crowd," he said. "They have good times."

"Mister, you're welcome to them."

He gave her a swift glance. "You know what they do, don't you?"

She shook her head. Sparkman licked his lips. "Those chains aren't for show. They work in parking lots, see. Then when they see a car they like, they clobber the guy, and sell it on the sly. They do other things too. They're wild."

"I'll bet."

He glanced at her leg. "You'd better put something on that," he said. "It was a good thing I was around."

"How come?"

He made a left hand turn. The other car was still behind them, but he didn't notice it. Neither did Allie.

"I said, how come."

"Oh, I thought maybe something might happen to you."

"I bet you loved that."

He gave her another piggy glance out of those black marbles of his. The car drew into a two story motel.

"Hey, where are we?"

"I thought we'd put something on that cut."

"Like an etching maybe?"

Sparkman chuckled and shook his head. "You don't understand me at all," he said. He sounded disappointed. "Sometimes

I don't think you know the ropes, exactly." He seemed obscurely excited and boyish. "Besides, maybe you could use a drink, huh?"

Allie was too worn out to say anything. He locked the car and led her upstairs, and around the open gallery to number thirty-two. He was nervous as a cat.

"You live here?" she asked, before she went in.

"Sometimes." He looked up and down the deserted gallery, and then followed her inside. Outside in the street came the sound of a car stopping. It was just an ordinary night noise. Neither one of them noticed it. He tapped the wall. "Soundproof. We have television too, only it isn't on now."

Allie thought he was quite a joker. She sat down while he went into the kitchenette to make a drink. She was a little awed. It was a ritzy motel. It had a gaudy magnolia wallpaper, the furniture was blond wood, and the rug was magnolia too. The TV faced the bed. She thought that was cozy. She liked luxury, and she thought this room was it. It soothed her. She was still on edge, but as long as he didn't try anything fancy, she thought she might as well relax.

But she still wanted to know why he had been there.

There was silence. She heard him getting ice out of the ice-box.

"Well, I thought I'd keep an eye on you," he said finally. He sounded bothered. "I knew that guy Sanducci would be round. He isn't the sort of man you should know."

"What's wrong with him?"

"There isn't anything wrong with him really." Sparkman sounded very cautious.

He came back with the drinks, and he had made them strong. He sat down beside her. He oozed confidence and security. "Sanducci's got his eye on you. You know that, don't you? He's always trying to muscle in on somebody's fun. And Purvis doesn't trust him. You're sort of caught in the middle. You know

Purvis? That boy who sings? At least he calls it singing. My, my." He clucked to himself and went on talking.

He talked to her like an uncle talking to a little girl. It was certainly a new approach. She knew it was a trick, but she found it soothing.

"You know I had a hunch Pedersen might turn up and try something like that." His eyes glittered. "It was a good thing I had it, wasn't it?"

It was late and she was sleepy. But Pedersen scared her, and suddenly the drinks didn't help. She still didn't feel safe. Her head was going too fast.

Sparkman was still excited. She wondered what he was so excited about. But she was beginning to care less. She thought he was a funny kind of man, but if he didn't want to do anything, that was okay with her. Some men didn't, she knew.

After about the third drink he went to the bathroom and came back with some hydrogen peroxide and a band-aid. He knelt down on the floor clumsily, to fix her leg. He wouldn't let her take her booties off, and he really made a production of it. She winced when he swobbed on the peroxide. No doubt he meant to be kind. Or did he?

There was something all wrong about him.

"It isn't very strong," he said. He sounded sad. It was funny. He gave her another drink. Then, she didn't know how much later, he began to show her his photographs.

He bent over them eagerly. He watched her sideways to see what she made of them.

She'd never seen photographs like that before. At first she was so busy trying to be sophisticated that she didn't really take them in. But when he went to the bathroom she leafed through them hurriedly. He seemed to stay away a long time. When he came back she'd gotten her breath again and asked him where he got them.

"I've got a camera," he said. He seemed suddenly shy. "You can earn money that way. You'd be good."

Allie was very drunk. She giggled. He looked at her hopefully. He was drunk himself. He went to the closet and staggered back with a big press Leica. "See," he said. "It's got a cable release. And I've got everything here."

Light was beginning to dawn. "Is that what Pedersen does?"

"He's got some films. He just delivers them for some guy. He never will tell me who." Sparkman's face darkened. "He charges too much. I don't like him."

Allie had lost her bearings. About two drinks later Sparkman had set up the camera. "One day I'd like to make films," he said. "I knew you'd do this sort of thing. Isn't that crazy? You can always tell. But there aren't many people who like it." He looked wistful again. Something creaked somewhere. Allie was clobbered.

He put down his drink and went back to the closet. When he came back he was carrying manacles, handcuffs and chains, in a sort of bundle. Allie looked at them.

"Hey, what's going on," she said.

Sparkman looked ready to cry. He undid one of the manacles and came towards her drunkenly.

She shoved him aside.

"You said you would."

"What are you anyway?" Allie demanded. She jumped up. Sparkman looked nasty. They stared at each other, and then he came forward again. She didn't know what she was doing. She grabbed at the chains and began to lash out with them. She must have hit him. He giggled. He cowered down on the floor. "Do it again," he muttered. "Harder."

It set Allie off. She began to beat him. She couldn't stop. Sparkman began to yell. He was big, fat and puffy, and the drink hadn't done him any good. The photographs slithered across the room. Allie slipped on them. Then she sort of went out of her head. She beat him again and again.

Suddenly Sparkman was lying very still on the floor. She stared at him with disbelief. She knew she had to get out of there.

He had made her do something she shouldn't have done. She didn't feel sorry. He was queer anyway. But she knew she had to get out, and she wasn't exactly inconspicuous. Maybe there was a coat in the closet. She pulled it open.

There wasn't a coat. But neatly hung up in a row was a line of women's dresses and slips. Allie just goggled. She turned to stare at Sparkman on the floor. He didn't move. She gasped, and then grabbed some clothes at random. Of course Sparkman was a fat man, but he wasn't tall. Five minutes later she was wearing a white silk slip with lace, better than she'd ever owned, and a print dress. It was too cold for the night air, but it was nicer than anything else there. She stood looking round the room. Then, on impulse she grabbed the camera. After all, he owed her something. There was even a cowhide bag to carry it in, and it looked as though it were worth plenty.

Sparkman lying there gave her the shudders. It was his fault, but she hoped he wasn't dead. She stood in the middle of the slithering photographs, swinging the camera while she caught her breath. Then she headed for the door.

It opened, and Sanducci came in.

"It was cold out there," he said. "I got tired of waiting. Someone should'a closed the venetian blind properly."

Allie gasped.

"Well, did you kill him?" Sanducci shut the door behind him, pocketed the key, and went over to Sparkman, frisking him expertly. When he straightened up Sparkman didn't have his wallet any more.

"He'll live," he said. He looked down at him, toeing the body. "He's getting sort of old for this." He glanced round the room, at the chains and the pictures. "I suppose I've got enough on him to run him in, now. I've been watching him for a long time, and my record could use it."

Allie backed towards the sofa, still clutching the camera. He eyed the camera, but he didn't say anything about it.

"Well?"

It was too much for Allie. Sanducci smiled. "Only this time I'm not going to. Do you know why?"

Allie shook her head.

"Because I've got you just exactly where I want you. You know that, don't you? I could run you in right now. It wouldn't matter what you said. The boys wouldn't listen to you anyway. Did you ever spend a night in the tank?"

Allie gripped the sofa. "What do you want?"

"Nothing yet." He looked round the room. "Ever seen anything like this before?"

Allie shook her head.

"As the man said, you travel in fast company. Maybe we could do something about that. You keep your mouth shut for a while, that's all."

"You don't want me."

Sanducci seemed amused. "Honey, I wouldn't touch you with a pair of tongs. But other people might feel differently." On the floor Sparkman groaned. "Come on. We'd better get out of here before jumbo wakes up, or he might miss his camera."

Allie clutched the Leica.

"Don't worry." Sanducci unlocked the door. "Keep it. Sell it and buy some clothes. You'll need some clothes, and that dress fits you like a mother hubbard. That may be okay for Purvis and his pals. It won't do for mine."

Allie hesitated.

"I said come on," snapped Sanducci and shoved her out the door. Then he drove her back to *The Florida*. "You're quitting the drive-in," he told her. "I'm not in any hurry. Take a few days off and get some rest."

"Why are you doing this?"

He shrugged. "You'll find out." He leaned over and pushed open the door on her side. "And remember, one peep out of you, and you land in the pokey. I don't think you'd like that much.

After all, the guy wasn't as alive as all that, and cameras can be traced. Go on, you're a mess. Get out."

Allie got.

He called her back, and handed her a bundle. "You'd make one hell of a criminal," he said. "You forgot your booties and stuff. Not that he'll squawk. He don't dare." He stared her down. "But don't kid yourself. One false step out of you, and I will."

CHAPTER ELEVEN

J ANEY was awake, and heard Allie come down the corridor to
her own room. She made no effort to go in to her. She didn't
want to see her, and hadn't seen her since they had both gone to
work.

Allie was the one Sparkman was interested in, so he had split
them up. Apparently he knew every shady hangout in town. The
job he'd gotten Janey was in a late show movie house, as an usherette in the balcony.

Janey hadn't liked that either. She'd liked the manager even
less. But the pay was $34.50 a week, and that was better than
going on the town, the way Allie wanted her to. At least so she
thought at first.

The movie house was called *The Broadway*. It was a narrow hole-in-the-wall off Market Street. Inside it was bigger than
it looked. It had no air-conditioning system, and played six
shows a day, so it stank with a sickening odor of stale cigarette
butts and human sweat. It had fluorescent girlie murals on the
walls and the wash rooms were always busy. It was that kind of
theatre.

Nor had she any way of knowing that the theatre was part
of Torrey's regular beat. It was one of the places he felt he had to
keep an eye on. Certainly somebody should have. She needn't
have worried. The first time he saw her there he didn't even recognize her.

That was because of the usherette's uniform. She hated it. The
manager was just the kind of man Sparkman would know. He

was oily and pale at the same time. He'd taken her into the girl's powder room and fished out a costume for her.

"This was Mabel's," he said. "She was about your size. She isn't with us any more."

Janey wondered what that meant. But she took the uniform. It was worn and sleezy. It felt tired. She looked around her.

The manager wanted to see what she'd got. He leaned against the wall, chewing a toothpick, and told her she could try it on right there. Janey wouldn't have that.

"We don't usually get your type girl," said the manager, and lolled back to the office. But when she came in with the uniform on he seemed to show a real interest. He was genuinely taken. That was what she didn't want.

She went to work right away.

She never did get to see the downstairs section, but the balcony was spooky. People were always moving around slowly. They prowled the aisles. The floozies came in pairs and were hard to take. Even so it took her a while before she caught on. She really was naïve. At first she thought they were just restless.

Then she began to notice things.

"For Pete's sake," said the manager angrily. He had hauled her on the carpet. "Never go up into the back rows waving that flashlight. What do you thing you are, a watch and ward society or something? You want to ruin me?"

She blushed. She couldn't think of anything to say.

"Okay," he said. "Okay. But they have to go somewhere, you see. Here they get a free movie, too. Now if you were a teetotaler you'd understand the attitude. Anything's better than beer."

He was in a good mood that day. That was the day he pinched her bottom hard.

She was glad the balcony was dark. So were the patrons. After a while she didn't mind them too much. Perhaps she was getting hardened. But she was careful not to look too close. There really wasn't much reason for her to be there, anyway. Nobody wanted to be shown to a seat. They just wanted to find a seat next to a seat with someone in it.

The pictures changed on Wednesdays, if the manager felt like it. They were horrible pictures. By the tenth time she had seen them, Janey didn't even look any more. Unfortunately that gave her time to worry.

The manager told her she wasn't very enterprising.

"What does that mean?"

He shrugged his shoulders. "Some guys like girls tricked up in monkey suits. I don't pay much. What do you think your youth is for?"

For instance, him. She hoped he wasn't being nasty about it. You could tell from his mouth he could be mean as hell. She edged away. She said she had to get back on duty.

He didn't like it, and yet it seemed to amuse him. He laughed. She didn't want to turn her back on him. The seat of her slacks was too shiny and too tight. And she didn't like getting pinched. She edged out of the office and went back to the balcony.

That was Wednesday. She was on duty Thursday when a man in black slacks and a white shirt open at the neck came up the stairs and took a seat well back. He was breathing heavily.

About fifteen minutes later two plainclothesmen came in. That wasn't unusual. They always patroled the theatre. But this time one of them was Torrey. She recognized him by his silhouette, before he saw her. She drew back. She didn't want him to see her here. But he did see her. He looked puzzled, and then he gave her a warm smile. It only lasted a second, but somehow it meant something. Then they marched up the aisle.

The man in the white shirt saw them coming. He didn't move. He sat there like a paralyzed bird. They reached his row and bent over him. There was a flurry of whispered talk. Then they marched him back down the aisle. When he passed Janey he spat. He must have thought she'd tipped them off. The other cop cuffed him on the side of the neck. She recognized the man now.

He was one of Purvis' gang. And he had recognized her, and she knew what he thought. That scared her. She had seen what Purvis did to Allie. And the others looked even tougher than Purvis.

Janey watched them go down the stairs. At the turn Torrey looked back at her. She flinched. She felt so ashamed of herself. But at least he had smiled at her as though he knew she existed. That helped a lot.

One thing, the gallery was quieter after that. Her nerves were on edge, so she was grateful for that. She didn't much care for walking back to the hotel at three A.M. through the dangerous streets. She looked behind her and walked a little faster. There wasn't even Allie to talk to. Allie didn't have time for anybody these days.

Torrey was in the theatre almost every night after that. He never said anything much. But he always acted as though he expected to see her, and he always smiled.

He was there because the heat was on. It made the tenderloin restless, but that was what he was there to watch. He got used to seeing her, and she knew he liked her. But he couldn't say much. He was always with his partner, and his partner was Sanducci. He didn't want Sanducci to get any ideas. So he would just nod and smile. It didn't go any farther than that.

The job made her feel hot and faded and tired. Whenever she came on duty the manager would be hanging round the lobby, waiting for his eyeful.

Friday he asked her to come into the office for a minute. She knew that he would get round to that eventually, and now he had. It was about one-thirty, and the night was sultry. There wasn't any air-conditioning in the theatre and she felt limp. She didn't dare not to go. She needed the money. Perhaps he would be kind.

He wasn't kind. He was too nervous to be kind, and that made him impatient. As soon as she got in the door, she knew what he was up to. But she didn't know what to do about it.

His name was Fred. She never did learn his last name. He made a point of being called Fred. He always wanted to be friends. She faced him wearily. He looked like an oversexed seal that has been left on the beach too long.

The office was tiny. It was probably smart once, back about 1936, but nobody had touched it since. It didn't have any windows, just drapes, draw drapes at that, over a blank section of the wall. The desk was a mess.

"What did you want to see me about?" she asked.

He was pretending to be busy. He looked up. He was trying to be pleasant, but actually he looked angry. Clearly he didn't want any nonsense out of her.

"I've been worried about you, Janey," he said. "You're an unusual girl. I don't think you're very happy with us."

"I've no complaints."

"But you don't get into the swing of the thing." He shot her a darting glance. "You got a boyfriend?"

"No." As soon as she said that, she knew she should have said yes. She watched him warily.

"At your age that isn't right. Or maybe you don't like kids. Maybe you like older men."

She thought about that. It was true. Torrey was older than she was. She always liked men like Torrey. But she never really knew them.

To herself she half nodded.

Fred looked relieved. He was eyeing her narrowly. "A lot of girls do. It's sensible. They feel safer. And then an older man knows more. He can do a lot for a girl." He played with a pile of letters. "You sure you closed that door?"

Janey nodded again. He hadn't asked her to sit down, and she didn't want to sit down.

"What's wrong with you now?" he demanded. "You see, this is a tough town. You need someone to look after you." He paused. "You understand what I mean?"

"I think so."

"Oh hell, you're the dumbest girl I ever saw," he said, and put the papers down.

Janey blinked.

He put his hands on the table, and pressed himself up out of his chair. He was a short man, and he had his clothes cut accordingly. They didn't make him look taller. They made him look like a burlesque comedian or something. Sparkman at least rolled round like a drunken senator. Fred pattered. He was vain of his feet. He wore narrow little printed shoes, that made his feet look like snakes. He came round the desk. She didn't move. He gripped her arms.

"Didn't Sparkman tell you anything?" he demanded. He sounded indignant. "I only want to help you." His little moustache quivered sadly.

She tried to wrench away. That made him smile. He held her more tightly. "Oh my," he said. "You're really something. I'm not so bad am I?"

He was stronger than he looked. She gave a sob. That made his eyes glitter.

"You're hurting me," she said. She eyed the door. That made him giggle. His teeth were too white to be real. He looked glazed. His eyes were vacant. He held her tight and began to pinch her bottom all over.

She screamed, and he put his hand over her mouth. He was really angry.

"What do you think you're doing? You got a friend out there, or something?" He eyed her more closely and he looked scared now. She tried to wrench away.

"That guy Sparkman's crazy," he said. "I should know better than to believe him any more." But he was excited. He wouldn't let go of her.

They were by the fake window. Janey bit his hand as hard as she could. He just held her tighter. She got an arm free, and managed to jerk one of the drapes. It was rotten at the top. It came away and she slung it over his head. It startled him. His grip relaxed. She wriggled away and made a dash for the door out into the lobby.

Sanduci and Torrey were just coming in, for a last checkup. Sanducci needed to haul somebody in, and was looking for a drunk or something, or a couple of hustlers. They always stayed out the last show.

She stood stock still in the middle of the lobby. Torrey looked past her into the office, where Fred was still struggling with the drape. Sanducci grinned.

Torrey came forward and took her arm. It was bruised. She flinched and looked up at him. Torrey didn't say anything. He headed for the door. He looked mad.

"Where are you going?" demanded Sanducci.

"I'm taking her home."

"You can't do that. It isn't any of your business."

Torrey didn't bother to say anything. He went straight on.

"Hey," said Sanducci. He paused. "Okay," he said. "I'll remember it."

"I don't give a damn what you remember." Torrey rushed her out under the marquee and up the street.

Janey felt awful. She practically died being out in the street in that getup. She didn't want to be seen like that.

"You shouldn't have done that," she said. "I don't want to cause any trouble. But thanks."

Torrey shrugged. "Somebody had to get you out of there."

They might have been brother and sister, the way they were talking. It was funny. She felt so at ease with him. But she knew better than to relax really. Her usherette's costume was old and thin and the street was cold.

Torrey walked her to the end of the block and waited for the light to change. He looked angry.

"I have to get back," he said. "You'll be okay now." He hesitated. "I wouldn't go back there, if I were you."

She knew she didn't have much choice, but it was nice of him. She knew what he meant. She felt flattered that he even remotely cared. "My clothes are there."

"You should never have come here in the first place." He shoved his hat farther back on his head and glowered at her. "Oh hell," he said, and smiled. "Take care of yourself. You're just a kid. This is tough stuff."

For a moment she thought he was going to touch her. But he didn't. He turned on his heel and walked back towards the theatre. She went on to the hotel. When she was in shadow, she glanced back, but the street was empty.

It made her sad. They could never really meet. It was silly to think they could. Somehow she'd got into a world where he couldn't even speak to her or she to him.

Sadly she went home to bed.

She dreaded going down to the theatre the next day, but she had to. Besides, it was payday. She put on her other dress, and carried the uniform under her arm.

She'd never been in the theatre in the afternoon before. She went early, hoping that Fred wouldn't be there. But he was. His office door was open. As soon as she let herself in, he came to the doorway.

"Well, what do you think you want?" he asked.

"I came for my clothes."

She must have winced. "You needn't worry," he snapped. "Why didn't you say you had cop friends?"

"He isn't a friend. He was just there."

"How do I know you're not a plant? The way they're cleaning up this town you could be anything."

She went into the powder room and got out her coat and dress, and put the uniform on the empty hook. When she came back he was still standing there, waiting for her.

"Do I come on duty tonight?" she asked. Her voice cracked. That was the question she had been dreading to ask. She needed the money so badly.

"Hell no, whatever you are, you're jail bait. I don't want you, you're fired."

She blinked. "What about my check for this week?"

"Try and get it," he snapped, went into his office, and slammed the door.

She went back to the hotel. She had all day to think about it. She had about a dollar and forty cents. That's why when Allie came in, even though she was awake, she didn't dare face her. She knew she wouldn't get any sympathy, and she needed sympathy bad. So she lay there in the dark, waiting for morning, until she fell asleep.

Torrey had such a nice voice.

CHAPTER TWELVE

Allie knew she was up a tree. She didn't care what she had done to Sparkman. He had had it coming, and besides, she wouldn't get caught. But Sanducci was another matter. Sanducci was right. He had her right where he wanted her.

Even back in Manteca, where nobody was very smart, you had to watch yourself with the police, and once they had something on you they never let you go. Allie knew about that. Manteca had a brothel on a side street. It paid a lot of protection. Just the same the girls had to be agreeable when the cops wanted them to be, and they didn't get paid for it, either.

And Sanducci was smart. He was up to something. The only way to get away from him was to get something on him. Allie had sharp eyes. Sometimes she saw more than was good for her. But from now on she'd have to find out everything she could.

In other words she was right back where she started from, only worse. It didn't make her feel any better. And bringing Janey was another mistake. Allie wasn't used to making mistakes. She didn't like it.

In addition to which she didn't have a cent until she hawked the camera. Tonight was pay day for Janey. She'd have to borrow some money from her.

Allie stayed in her room all that day. Janey had to go to work at six. Six came and went, and Allie didn't hear her go down the corridor. That puzzled her. It almost pleased her. Maybe Janey had wised up and got herself someone to play with. It was about time. She got up to go into Janey's room and see. She really did expect it to be empty.

She unlocked the connecting door and went in.

The room wasn't empty. Janey was lying in the dark, on the bed, with a blanket over her. Allie decided to be tender. She sat down on the bed and shook her gently.

"Hey, wake up," she said. "You're late for the theatre."

"I'm not asleep." Janey did not stir.

"I thought you got paid today. I'm broke."

"Oh."

"Is that all you've got to say, oh?"

Janey turned over in the bed. She didn't want to look at Allie and she didn't want Allie to see her. She didn't want to be seen by anyone. It was the end of the month. She had found something out, and it didn't make her feel any friendlier towards Allie or anyone else. Sometimes she wondered whether Allie was her friend or not.

Allie stared at her impatiently. There were times when Janey wouldn't do what she wanted her to do. She dug her heels in, and it was hard to tell why.

"What about the drive-in?" Janey said after a while.

"Well, what about it?"

"I thought you were working there."

"That's for squares," said Allie. She peered over at her. "Haven't you got any money at all?"

"A dollar fifty. He fired me. He wouldn't pay."

"Well, I'm not going to keep you. I can't even keep myself. If no one will hire you, you've just got to get out and land some dope."

"We can't go back to the Jickey Room."

"Who said *we* have to? *You* have to. I'm just not going to carry you any more, that's all."

Mention of the Jickey Room made Allie nervous. She was afraid of Purvis herself. And with Sanducci stalking her from the other end, that didn't leave her much room. She needed help.

So Allie decided to be sweet. She could be overwhelmingly sweet when she wanted to be. She usually got what she wanted with vinegar, but she was good with sugar too. Her voice became saccharine. Janey could just feel her sweetening up. It didn't take her in any more, but Allie couldn't know that.

Besides, Allie wasn't being faky. She never thought about things like that. She just automatically tried to get her own way, and if one system didn't work then she tried another.

"You're sick today," she said. "You can go back to the movie house tomorrow."

"I'll never go back there." Janey pulled herself up in bed. She was so angry with Allie she could cry.

Allie shrugged. "You have to eat."

"I don't have to eat and I'm not sick."

"Well, I do. Give me your dollar fifty. After all, I've carried you long enough. It's your turn to carry me."

"I said I'm not sick," said Janey. Her eyes sparkled dangerously.

Allie was reaching for the purse. She put it down. Maybe she knew what was coming. It had been bound to come some time, but she'd forgotten about it. She looked annoyed.

"I'm not pregnant," said Janey. "I never was. What's more, you knew I never was."

Allie hesitated. "I was trying to help you, that's all. You're my best friend, aren't you?"

"Am I?"

The two girls stared at each other. Allie was the first to flush.

"So what?" she asked. "These things are tricky. Didn't anybody ever tell you the facts of life? Somebody had to get you out of that hick town."

"I liked that hick town."

Allie shrugged. "So you got knocked up by an apricot picker. So what? You want to go back to him or something?" Her voice had turned hard.

"I told you it was an accident. He wouldn't let me go. He trapped me. He was so big."

"Yeah, your aunt would believe that, wouldn't she?"

"It may be a hick town, but it's better than this life."

Allie sniffed. "Well, you know what you can do about that."

"I'm going home."

Allie blinked. That startled her. She didn't want Janey hanging round her neck, but she didn't want her out of the way either. "You haven't got a home to go to."

"I can work."

"You think they don't all know why you had to leave town?"

"They don't unless you told them."

Allie bit her nails. She looked embarrassed. "I did tell them."

"What?"

"Well, you were always so prim and proper and everything. And you know how it is. A guy takes you out and you talk. I didn't mean anything. You'd never have come, otherwise."

Janey merely stared at her.

"So you see it doesn't make any difference," Allie told her lamely.

"But you *tricked* me."

"I just wanted you to come along." Allie plucked at the coverlet, where the pattern was frayed away. "It wouldn't have been any fun alone."

"You call this fun?" Janey looked at her with disbelief.

"We're having a dead spot," admitted Allie. "Besides, I can't do anything until my face is better. But you're pretty. You could have anyone you wanted."

"I won't do it." Janey hit the coverlet with her fists.

"You thought it was a fun-idea when we started."

"I don't know what I thought. I thought I was pregnant. I had to do something."

"But it's fun," said Allie. "How do you know till you've tried?"

"I've tried," said Janey bitterly.

"That guy in Manteca? He was just an Okie or something. He wasn't nothing."

"You like Purvis better?" demanded Janey. "Do you think I want to do that sort of thing. I want to be clean and decent and not have people pawing me all the time."

Allie looked at her for a long time. "You're crazy," she said. "From now on you fend for yourself. I'm taking fifty cents. I have to go somewhere. That leaves you a buck. It'll buy you a couple of drinks while you get started." She was red in the face. She reached for the purse again, and Janey didn't try to stop her. "Okay. So I played you a dirty trick. You should be glad you're not stuck with a brat. Didn't you ever play a dirty trick on anyone? Sometimes you have to." She stopped in the doorway. "You think you're so damn good. You just make me plain tired."

She opened the door and stopped again. "I mean it," she said. "I'm not giving you a cent."

Janey knew she meant it. But there wasn't anything to say. The door banged, and she was left alone. She knew why she meant it, too. Allie never forgave anyone who found her out. When that happened, she might pretend to be polite, but she was through.

CHAPTER THIRTEEN

A LLIE went off to hock the camera, before anybody tried to check the serial number. She was furious. She never wanted to speak to Janey again. She was so mad she didn't even notice she was being followed. Pedersen and Purvis did. They drew back and gave up for the time being. It was night. That hid them.

Janey stayed in her room. If there had been a radio or something that would have helped, but there wasn't any radio. She had to make a decision. Yet she could make no decision. She kept hoping that Allie would come back, but Allie didn't come back. The hotel seemed very empty.

The point was, what did she do now?

It wasn't a moral matter. It was a question of eating or starving. At around ten she forced herself to get up and dressed slowly. Then she left the hotel and glanced up and down the street uncertainly. She felt horribly old. It seemed hard to believe she was only eighteen. Yet when she caught sight of herself in store mirrors, it was a fresh faced girl who looked back at her, as though mocking her. It made her wince.

The streets were very quiet. The clean up campaign was in high gear. Everyone who hadn't been hauled in by the cops knew better than to risk hustling on the streets. Nobody ever knew what all that sudden virtue was for, but it always came around at least once a year. Maybe it helped sell newspapers. But it made Janey nervous. She thought she looked so obvious, what she was up to and everything, and all she needed was a session in night-court. Allie might be able to handle that. She couldn't.

As she went past Bob and Anna's she hesitated, feeling the dollar in her purse. She was hungry. But if she spent her last dollar she'd have no more dollar to spend. She felt too shabby to go to a new bar. So she wound up outside the Jickey Club. At least there wasn't much danger of that being raided. It was heavily protected. Sanducci saw to that.

The only way to face it out was to breeze right in, so that was what she did. At first the place made her blink. She had forgotten Torrey might be there, and she'd die of shame if he saw her working on the customers. She couldn't face the bar right away. Fortunately the place was crowded. Nobody had noticed her. The five-piece band was going full blast. She wormed her way down the length of the room to the ladies room. She couldn't hide there forever, but she needed time to adjust.

When she came out again she felt better, but not for long. The rear of the Jickey Club was shadowy, and widened out. Between the dais and the wall there was enough room for a couple of booths. Beer cases were stacked against the entry to the lavatories. She saw Pedersen slouch heavily into one of the booths, with Purvis behind him. She did not know why she drew back to listen, but she did. Certainly she didn't want them to see her, and to get back to the main room she'd have to pass right in front of them. But from where she was she could see into the booth.

Pedersen hauled his boots up on the table, wriggled them, and jerked his cap down over his head. It made him look like a village idiot.

"She got away," he said.

The Italian girl, Vera, was sitting opposite him. She stared at his boots with distaste and then slid away. "I don't see what you want her for anyway," she snapped. "She's nothing but trouble."

"That's why we wanted her."

"Hell, she beat Pedersen up," said Purvis. "I don't like my friends beat up."

"What happened?"

Pedersen shrugged. "Sparkman picked her up, so she got away. Then Sanducci followed her. To Sparkman's I mean. I went up afterwards. They sure laid him low."

"That doesn't prove anything."

"What do you know what Sparkman might say? He shakes like blubber. They just about killed him. I tell you she's in with Sanducci, and Sanducci's tricky."

Vera shifted in her seat. She looked uncomfortable. "I told you you don't have to worry about Sparkman."

"Then why's he seeing the girl?"

"Maybe he likes her."

"Him?" Purvis was contemptuous. "Sparkman never got no stuff from us. Nothing but the pictures, and who cares about them. But she might know more than we think. Hell, we can't take a chance."

"What did you tell her?" demanded Vera.

"What do I know what I tell her? I get excited I could say anything, you know that. All you have to do is ask me."

Vera leaned across the table and stared at him. "Did she ask you?"

"Not that I remember. But hey, we gotta get her. She beat Pedersen up here, with that damn chain of his. I notice he's not wearing it now."

"Well, you've got to go sort of quiet with the heat on," said Pedersen. "I've got other things."

"I'll bet," said Vera.

Purvis hunched forward. His eyes sparkled. "We were following her tonight, see. We thought we'd take her out, well, you know where. Put a scare into her. But that damn cop was shadowing her. So we came here."

"I told you that doesn't prove anything," snapped Vera.

"I said he was following her. He's protecting her," snarled Pedersen.

"What do you want to do, cut her up?" asked Vera. "Or are you just scared?"

Pedersen took his feet down. "I don't scare."

Vera just laughed, and as she jerked her head, Janey caught her eye. She couldn't know whether she'd been spotted or not. She didn't understand.

Pedersen got up, and Purvis followed him. Vera held Purvis back, while Pedersen clomped out of the bar.

"He's gotta make a delivery," said Purvis.

"Why don't you get rid of that goon?"

Purvis shrugged. "He's my protection. Besides, when he gets her, he's going to beat her up good. Come and watch."

Vera held his arm. "Do you really think she knows anything?" Vera seemed suddenly uneasy.

Purvis made a face and sauntered off into the crowd. Vera tagged after him.

Janey came out of hiding and moved towards the bar. Vera must have seen her, and that didn't make Janey feel any easier. They were a scarey bunch. She wedged herself into the bar, on a stool near the door. She heard a servicycle start up outside. That would be Pedersen. Vera didn't come back. Two policemen came in, neither of them Torrey. They looked round and then went over and talked to the bartender. The bartender looked angry, and then resigned.

The girl next to Janey was watching the bartender. She slipped off her stool and ambled towards the door. She ambled fast, while the cops still had their backs turned. Janey followed at once. She didn't know why. She just did. Her heart was in her stomach.

Outside, out of the corner of her eye, she saw a patrol wagon down the street. There was a doorway next to the Jickey Club. Quickly she sank back into it. She was just in time. The girl in front of her walked smack into a policeman.

Janey shook. She leaned back, and the door behind her gave. She opened it and backed into a dark smelly hallway. Someone was standing there. Janey gasped and whirled around.

It was Vera. They stared at each other wordlessly. Then Vera shrugged. "Come upstairs," she said. "The view's better."

She turned and marched up the stairs. Janey couldn't stay where she was. She followed. Outside someone blew a whistle. Vera ran faster.

The building was an old office loft, dating from the first World War, for rent, and abandoned. The stores on street level were a jewelry pitch and a newspaper and pinball and shoeshine place. But they hadn't been able to rent the upstairs. There was litter on the floor. Vera tried a door and pushed it open. It squeaked.

Janey stood stock still.

"In here," said Vera impatiently. Janey followed. They stood in the loft at the front of the building. It was a mess of abandoned furniture and old newspapers. Vera went over to the window. They both did. They looked down.

The wagon had pulled up to the door. Some of the crowd on Market had stopped to look, but somehow the street was emptier than it had been.

Janey drew back. Vera took her by the back of her neck and pushed her forward. "I've had enough of you two," she said. "Look."

Janey looked.

The cops were taking the B-girls out. They seemed embarrassed about it and they'd only taken a few. No doubt the place would be closed up for a day or two, and then reopen later. That was the way with a place as well protected as the Jickey Club. But the girls were worse than embarrassed. For them it was real trouble. They were used to it, most of them, but that didn't make it any easier for them.

Janey shivered. Another two minutes and she'd have been one of them. The girls weren't even angry. They just let themselves be herded along into the wagon. Out in the streetlight they looked older and uglier than they really were. One of them was a girl her own age, but how had her face gotten that hard?

"They almost nabbed me," said Vera. "Me!"

Janey didn't say anything. The loft was clammy and cold. Her suit was very thin.

"All I can say is, it's a damn good thing Purvis and Pedersen got away, or I'd cut you up myself," said Vera. "What were you listening in back there for?"

"I wasn't...."

"I saw you. Were you getting something juicy for your little friend's cop? I guess you know now what'll happen to her, if she was in on this."

"But I didn't.... I just got away myself."

"They could have let you. That would look good. What do we know about you anyway?" Vera was rattled.

"But I don't know anything," sobbed Janey.

Vera looked her up and down coolly. "Well, that's what I thought," she said, "but you never know." She looked down into the street. "Come on."

"Where?"

"I've got to think this over," said Vera. "Come on." She stood to one side. "They're gone now. The coast is clear." She didn't give Janey any chance to do anything but follow. She pushed her ahead of her down the stairs, and back to the bar.

Maybe the matter wasn't so serious, for they'd raided early, when there wasn't much chance of making much of a haul. But it was bad for business, and they might have gotten something else. At least that's what Vera kept saying. The crowd in the bar had thinned out, but the place wasn't exactly emptied. The timid rabbits would be frightened off, and that's where the girls made the cash. The hardened regulars were still there. They were used to people disappearing for a while.

The far end of the bar was deserted. Vera made right for it, and sat Janey down between her and the wall, so she couldn't get out. Then she waited.

After a while Sam, the senior bartender, noticed her and sort of drifted down her end. He put his elbows on the bar and looked at her. He looked sad. If the cops dragged the bartenders in for serving minors or anything, he was the one who had to take the rap. He got paid off for it, but once in a while you ran into a tough judge, and he didn't like the inside of a jail well enough to look forward to thirty days in it. Besides he had a family, and he liked to spend his days off with his kids.

"Well, what's the story," asked Vera.

"Search me. They just came in and dragged the girls out."

"Nobody else," asked Vera quickly.

Sam glanced at Janey and mopped the bar with a plastic square. Then he shook his head.

"What'd they say?"

"They said they'd keep it quiet. They did. They were real orderly. I don't think Sanducci was double crossing us or anything. These things happen. Hell, suppose they got tough and closed us up? Or they caught Pedersen with a load?"

Vera shut him up quick. She just stared him down.

"But who tipped them off?" she asked.

Sam looked at Janey. "What about the girl? She hasn't been round long. Purvis and Pedersen think that friend of hers is up to something."

Janey shrank into herself. She couldn't look at them.

"Think any of the girls will talk?"

Sam shrugged. "They've got their living to earn. And they're all regulars."

"Well, that leaves you," said Vera, and swung round to Janey. "And what you are, we'll just have to wait and see."

Sam watched her.

"Go away," said Vera. "Miss Muffit and I here have to have a little private talk."

Sam went.

Vera stared at Janey for quite some time. Then she smiled. An idea had hit her. It wasn't a nice smile. It was the sort of smile Janey had seen on Allie's face sometimes. It was scornful and cruel, and foxy.

"You came here to hustle, you say," said Vera.

Janey hesitated and then nodded. It was such an ugly word.

"Okay," said Vera. "We'll give you a chance to prove it."

Janey didn't say anything, but her eyes widened.

"Well?" demanded Vera. "Oh I know your type. You like to look on and feel better than anybody else. Like that Torrey character." She looked at Janey sharply. "Yeah, that went home didn't it? You think I'm blind or something?" She put her head on one side. "Or is there maybe more in that than I think?"

Janey shook her head. She must have looked terribly pale. Vera chuckled. "Okay," she said. "You can't say you didn't ask for it." She motioned to Sam. "Keep an eye on her. I've got to make a phone call."

She toddled towards the booths, with that strangely Oriental walk of hers. Sam was as good as his word. He kept an eye on Janey. But he didn't say anything. She supposed she could have made a run for the door, but that only meant Pedersen would be turned loose on her.

She waited miserably. Sam saw that and grinned. He seemed to know what was coming. Janey felt her fingers sweating. She looked towards the door. She would have tried to get out, if there had been anywhere to go.

Vera came back. She looked more self-possessed now and more amused. "Come along," she said. She walked Janey out to the street, and hailed a cab.

Janey had never been in a cab before. She was tense and awed. The cab went down Market Street and then turned up Grant Avenue and entered Chinatown.

"I gues you know what business I'm in by now," said Vera. She looked out the window. "I have what you might call a specialized clientele. They pay better and they keep their mouths shut." She rapped on the driver's back and whispered something to him. "I made two phone calls," she said, looking out the rear window. "In case you get any fancy ideas."

The cab turned uphill and then turned into a narrow alley of tall buildings with iron balconies. Chinese music floated down to them.

"Social clubs," said Vera. They got out and stood for a moment on the sidewalk. The buildings were really tenements with enormous flights of inside stairs.

"What do I do?" demanded Janey. The neighborhood was creepy.

"That depends on what the guys want. And you know what'll happen to you if you don't. It won't be so bad. These guys who have funny ideas, they're generous if you string along with them."

They went up the stairs, to the second floor. The place was heavy with Chinese cooking smells. They were let into a dingy apartment. A Japanese scroll hung on the wall, or maybe it was Chinese. The rest of the furniture was pure Grand Rapids. For a moment they were alone. Then a man came through the far door.

He was short and squat and moonfaced, but the moon had shriveled up and grown flabby. He was oily and affable and eager. His teeth were small, flat, and deeply stained. He didn't walk, he floated.

"I'll wait here," said Vera.

The Chinaman looked surprised. He broke into a torrent of Chinese. It sounded like a teletype backfiring.

"I said I'd wait," said Vera firmly. "After all, she's new."

The Chinese brightened. Janey flinched, but she was trapped. He led her into an inner room, and there was nothing she could do but follow. She was half-way glad. There are times when you get so upset you long for something awful to happen to you. The Chinese was being soothing. He might have been a surgeon smoothing down a patient the night before an operation. She steeled herself to go through with it.

Then she saw the bed. The whole room was filled by the bed. It was the biggest bed in the world. It was built like a covered wagon. Three steps led up to it. Over it arched two hores-shoe arches, and the roof was lined with little mirrors. It was wood carved all over with mother of pearl eyes and ivory fangs.

He began to make gestures. She couldn't stand that. She wormed away from him. "I can't," she said. "I can't." She could hear her voice break.

He smiled and made clucking noises. But he went on. She ran. There was only one door, and she knew Vera was on the other side of it, but she just couldn't face him.

He ran after her.

As she came into the outer room, Vera was standing up. She took one look at Janey.

"That's about what I thought," she said.

The Chinese was angry. But Vera cut him off. "There won't be any charge," she said. "It was worth it just to find out. I thought little Miss Marker here was a fake."

Janey was trembling. "What are you going to do now?"

"We sit," said Vera. "I thought I'd have another little surprise ready for you, just in case I was right."

The Chinese didn't like that, but Vera spoke to him again. Janey didn't know what she said. Perhaps it was Chinese. She was too hysterical to know. At least the Chinaman went away. Vera smiled. "Nice, isn't he?" she said. She lapsed into silence, and sat watching Janey. Perhaps fifteen minutes went by. Janey knew she had to keep a grip on herself. But she wasn't succeeding very well.

The bell rang. Apparently Vera had been expecting it. She gathered up her purse and coat and they went down the stairs. Janey could see a shadow waiting on the other side of the glass. It wasn't very well outlined. Vera opened the door and shoved Janey out, right into Pedersen.

"Well, what gives?" he demanded.

"Where's Purvis?"

"He's in the car."

"I've been going over her credentials," said Vera. "She doesn't have any."

The car was a beat-up Studebaker. Vera shoved Janey in the back with Pedersen, and got in with Purvis. "Drive around a while," she said. "Did you phone the studio?"

Purvis nodded.

Janey huddled in the back seat, as far away from Pedersen as she could get. His clothes were smelly. And she knew what he'd tried to do to Allie. She could sense that he was tense and excited. He reached in the turn up of his jeans and pulled out a small black click knife. He clicked it in and out.

"You behave yourself," he said.

Janey was too scared to do anything else. The car might be beat up but it had power. It slipped smoothly in and out of traffic.

"Well, she's a fake all right, but what else she is I don't know," said Vera. "She could have tipped the raid. Her little friend is in deep with Sanducci. But that doesn't mean anything. It's Torrey that gets me."

Purvis stroked his cheek. "Yeah," he said. "Torrey's the one we gotta watch. But I thought Sanducci was watching him."

"Sanducci's been sitting pretty so long he doesn't know enough to open his eyes," said Vera.

Purvis jerked towards the rear seat. "What do you want to do with her?"

Vera shrugged. "I'd like to have something on her, and she's the home town type."

"So?"

"Let's turn her loose on Pop."

"That's sort of dangerous. She might not cooperate."

"Pedersen can see to that."

Purvis twisted round and looked in the back seat. Then he grinned. "That's real crazy," he said. "I guess he can, at that. But ain't she kind of thin?"

Velli shrugged. "Who cares? Some like them thin."

Purvis hummed under his breath and shoved the car across Market, down into the slums.

CHAPTER FOURTEEN

THE CAR turned off Mission Street into a dark alley, between warehouses and office buildings. At this hour of the night the streets looked kind of discouraged. The four of them got out of the car and Purvis unlocked a door. They were in the storeroom of a shop. There was almost no light. Pedersen nudged Janey ahead of him. They stood still for a moment, until their eyes adjusted. Then they saw some light under a farther door and headed for that. When Purvis got it open a flood of light came up from the head of a flight of stairs. They started down.

"He's here all right," said Purvis. "But then he always is, isn't he?"

They clattered down the stairs. When they reached the bottom a bent up fat man was scurrying around at a file cabinet.

"I guess we scared you, Pop. They wouldn't raid this place. They don't even know it's here," said Purvis.

Pop was angry. "You shouldn't come barging in here this way."

"You should be grateful. We brought you a model."

Pop came out under the overhead light. Janey knew where she was now. This was where they'd gotten their faked identity cards. She knew what she was here for, too. She remembered the tail end of that film Pop had run off.

Pop looked at her and grunted. "What you kids up to, bringing someone in here?"

"She won't complain," said Purvis. "She sorta needs the work."

"I can't get anybody else at this hour."

"We thought we'd build her up gradual like. Or maybe Pedersen might oblige."

Pop thought about it. Then it seemed to strike him as a good idea. But he was still grudging. "We could use a few stills, I guess," he said. "Pedersen and a girl, they might go for that. But are you sure she's safe?"

"She'll be safe," snapped Vera. Janey shivered. She didn't have much choice.

Pop's eyes narrowed. "Three bucks a still," he said. "The ones we use, that is."

Vera shrugged.

"It'll take me a while to get set up." He hesitated. "Out at the place we could take maybe some footage."

"Later, Pop."

"Stills are okay," said Pop. "They sell. But a movie would go over big." He looked Pedersen up and down. "She looks scared enough. We'll do that kind." He rustled off towards the far end of the basement.

Pop bustled round, turning on lights, arranging reflectors, and setting up the cameras. Vera, Pedersen, Janey and Purvis sat on a packing case and watched. They didn't say anything. There wasn't much to say.

Pop was one of those guys who make their living out of art. The art varies, but is always peculiar. So was Pop. He'd been everything from a tattoo specialist to short order cook. Now he made pornographic movies and the sort of stills some people keep in a bottom drawer. Pedersen delivered the movies and sometimes the stills, particularly those Pop made to order. He had quite a client list, but he kept it in his head. He'd been raided before, but never for this. The sort of films he made he got a hundred bucks a night for. He also made copies of older films. Those rented cheaper. The stills were all on his own, and if he let loose on blackmail once or twice, that was just luck. The sort of people who posed for him didn't usually get enough cash together to be worth blackmailing. But he was artistic. He liked hard-focus photography and everything just so. It took him a while to get ready.

"Okay," he said at last. He squinted round at them. "What's your name?"

"Janey," faltered Janey.

"Okay, Janey, take your clothes off."

Janey didn't move.

"She's sort of bashful, Pop," said Pedersen. "I'll take care of it."

They made her take her clothes off, all except her panties, while Pedersen lolled against a packing case, playing with his knife. Pop tossed her a dusty old negligee that could have fitted anybody. She was dying of embarrassment. She put it on.

"Let's set up a series," said Pop. "You're lying there, see, on that couch, doing your nails or something. One shot. Then he busts in. You're terrified. He attacks you. Then you like it. Then he does something real mean. Maybe five shots."

They herded her onto the couch. The lights made the rest of the basement darker. Purvis and Vera watched. Pedersen liked the whole deal. He liked swaggering in front of an audience. He was wearing a torn t-shirt, but it was one of those narrow weight-lifting t-shirts that show every muscle, and though he was scrawny, he had big arms. He still had his cap shoved on back of his head.

Janey just shut her eyes, gulped, and went through with it. It was a nightmare, but she thought maybe if she did what they told her to, they'd let her go eventually. Pedersen kicked her with his boots. They left bruises. That was supposed to be an accident. And for that first embrace, she really did fight.

Pop said that shot wasn't any good. If she was going to thrash round that way he needed a faster shutter speed and a diagonal shot with the camera. Then he decided he wanted to shoot low.

Purvis and Vera didn't say anything.

The session went on for two or three hours. Pedersen was excited now. He was hard to handle. He wanted to make the thing authentic. Once, in the third picture, Pop said she didn't have any expression. Pedersen grinned and knicked her with the knife. Not even Pop saw it. But it worked.

Pop was pleased. "They'll sell like hotcakes," she said. "She's good. She's virginal. You keep her round."

Pedersen grinned. "She'll be round," he said. "Where would she go?"

Janey was beginning to get the shakes. She couldn't stop. Pedersen hauled off and slapped her. Pop clicked the camera. "Fine," he said. "Fine."

Then they let her alone. She was barely conscious. She just sat on the sofa, huddled up in what was left of the negligee. At least it wasn't real. At least it was only a picture.

Vera told her to dress. She dressed. They left, but not before Vera had got the fee out of Pop. She took half the money, but she gave Janey the other half. It wasn't enough to run away on.

"Now we've got something on you," she said. "Those pictures would look real good back home. Or down at the police, maybe." She seemed to think it was funny. She really looked amused. So did Pedersen. So did Purvis. They went out to the street.

"So you see going to the police wouldn't do you any good, in case you had ideas. From now on you work here. Try anything and you know what'll happen."

Janey just nodded. She didn't much care. She felt dirty all over. In a way it was worse than the Chinese would have been, or any of the things Allie did. She'd get away from them when she could. But she was too worn out to do anything now, and besides, what could she do? Her half of the fee had been seven-fifty. She couldn't get far on that. And probably they'd watch her.

They dropped her at her hotel. "We'll be seeing you," they said. "It might not be such a good idea to go out for a while." They thought they had her right where they wanted her. And they were right. As far as she could see, they had.

CHAPTER FIFTEEN

A LLIE couldn't pawn the camera. She tried all the pawn shops and junk stores on Third Street, which was the right place to take things like that. The owners liked the camera, but they were afraid to take it. It might be hot. It could be traced. Maybe her manner was wrong. The police were trying to make a record for themselves. Nobody wanted to be caught out. Most of the dealers shot her out of the shop fast. One or two were more considerate. But coming in that way late at night, she couldn't expect them to take a chance. She had thirty cents and that was all. Having the camera was like having a check you couldn't cash.

She stood on the street. It was perhaps the first time the city had really frightened her. With Janey around she could feel grown up and sophisticated. But now Janey blamed her for everything. Right now Allie didn't feel grown up or sophisticated at all.

She was in the worst part of town, not the most criminal, but the part that looked the worst. She was in the boneyard. She was on skid row. Always before she'd been able to get by somehow. Someone or something had always turned up. But a city isn't like a small town. Unless you have enough cash to move around, you lose your footing in a city.

There were so many shapeless middle-aged drunks around, that even the sidewalks smelled of muscatel. She couldn't stand that section another five minutes. She walked up to Market, and faced the length of the street. In other moods she might have found it exciting. She liked a lot of people milling around and looking at her. She liked adventures. But right now she was flat broke. She didn't feel eager. She wanted to run for cover. It was just possible Janey might have some money. She went back to the hotel.

But Janey wasn't there.

Allie knew she'd have to go out later, but not right now. She put the camera on the bureau. It even had film in it. But she wasn't in the mood for taking pictures. She sat down on the bed and thought things over. As she noticed a run in her stocking the door opened and Sanducci edged into the room and shut the door behind him. He was in uniform this time. If anything he looked worse in uniform than he did in plain clothes. He had sallow, shadowy eyes.

"You didn't make out so good," he said, "now did you?"

"What did you mean by that?"

"I was tailing you. I told you you and me would have to have a little talk."

Allie looked up at him. There was no way of getting rid of him. So she listened. Walking home, she had noticed the patrol cars cruising along real slow. She'd seen girls shoved into the van before. She knew she had to listen. But she didn't have to like it.

Sanducci wasn't a man to waste time. But that didn't mean that he minded playing his fish a little, once he had it hooked. Being built the way he was, he had to get his fun somehow.

"About what?" asked Allie.

"This and that," he said. He snapped his fingers. "You haven't got a dime. I could maybe help you out."

"Why should you?"

"I got friends," he said. "You could maybe do them a favor. Of course I get my cut."

"Oh sure." Allie looked up at him. Sometimes when she was cornered she looked like an animal. "No thanks. I'd rather go back to the Jickey Club. That way nobody gets a cut."

Sanducci leaned against the wall. "You're so stupid you're wonderful," he said. "You can't go back there. Just try it. Don't you know Pedersen and Purvis are after you? I guess you know what they'd do to you. They think you're a stool for me. They think maybe I've got the wind up and want to turn them in. Maybe I do."

"For you?"

"Sure. We know better. But they don't. They don't like stools. Those boys are mighty jumpy these days. They're just itching to beat somebody up."

"Purvis likes me."

"Purvis was shaping you up. He lives off pimping. He doesn't like anybody. He certainly doesn't like you now."

"The Jickey isn't the only place."

"It will be by the time they get through cleaning up this town. If you want to go there, go ahead and try it. But don't say I didn't warn you."

"You haven't got anything on me."

"I don't need it. Maybe you'd like an example. Maybe you'd like to spend the night in the tank? Do you know what the tank is? I thought maybe you might. Some of those matrons just love working over a girl like you. They're spinsters. They've really got a grudge."

"What do you want me to do?" asked Allie sharply.

Sanducci shrugged. "A girl like you, young, you know, and not too stiff. She could make some cash quick. Real ritzy stuff. Not the stuff Purvis could get you. Not just these buy me a drink and come up for half an hour deals. You've been through the ropes. You know."

"I've never been through those ropes, brother."

He slapped her. "You don't speak to me that way. You go through any ropes I tell you to."

"I'm not listening."

"Okay. Find out for yourself. I offer you a good deal. Next time it may not be so good."

"What does that mean?"

"Like I said, find out for yourself."

"You're not sitting so pretty," said Allie. "You can't boss me around."

He whirled on her. "What do you mean by that?"

She flinched but she went on. "I got eyes. You've got your finger in this mess somewhere. You might get stuck someday."

He began to shake her. He shook her too hard. "What do you know?" he demanded. "What do you know?"

She laughed at him.

"I could break your neck real easy."

"That would look fine in the papers."

He knocked her against the wall. The doorknob to the closet bit into her kidney. "Talk," he said. He was livid.

She was really scared. She broke away. She ran for the door, got it open, and dashed down the corridor. He started to follow, and then slowed down. He kept his distance behind her. He knew what she'd find in the street. He ought to. He'd planted it there.

She went out into the street. She was mad and scared. She didn't see very well. He was still behind her. She doubled down an alley. Behind her she heard his car start up, but she couldn't remember what kind of car it was. On the next street over, she looked around, but everything seemed all right. She slowed down.

It was on the next corner that she caught somebody's eye. He began to follow her. She was annoyed and then relieved. She dawdled, trying to see him out of the corner of her eye or in a shop window. Finally she caught him reflected in the glass of a Chinese herbalist's. She was surprised. He was a little old, almost thirty-five, she thought, but he looked clean and nice. Luck went that way sometimes. He was staring in the glass, too. She smiled, and both their reflections smiled in the glass a little uncertainly. She relaxed. She knew what to do now. She forgot about things. She felt almost cheerful, just because he looked so nice and clean.

She walked deliberately under a street light, giggling to herself. He seemed shy. She waited, but he didn't catch up. She had to do something. She'd been with shy men before. They just died to speak to you, but they didn't know how. You had to make it easy for them. Once you began, they picked up the ball right away. And shy men were the generous ones. They were decent about things.

She stepped off the curb and pretended to turn her ankle. She was excited. It always excited her, even when she had first done it, when she was fifteen. She was just built that way. He offered to help her. He took her arm. She smiled at him shyly. After all, she was no tart. She was a young kid that was all. Perhaps a slight look in the eyes, to let him know she wasn't as young as all that. She began to tell him she was alone in town.

It went swell. She said she was a little broke. He understood. He was a little broke himself. She said that was all right, because she didn't worry about things like that. He'd cough up something eventually. Then she asked him if he wanted to come up.

"And do what?" he asked. He was very soft spoken.

"What do you think?" she asked. Maybe she was getting a little impatient. It was cold out there. She told him what she meant. He seemed to take it calmly. He asked her how much. That threw her off balance, but she said ten bucks.

He opened his coat and pulled a badge on her.

That had never happened to her in her whole life. She stood there, wide-mouthed, but before she could run, he had taken her arm.

"Oh mister," she said. "You can't do this."

"Girlie, I got orders."

"But I didn't mean anything."

"No, of course you didn't. Come on."

A brown sedan pulled into the curb. Sanducci got out. The plainclothesman looked at him uncertainly. Sanducci took out his wallet and showed him his Vice Detail Indentification. "It's okay," he said. "I'll take care of it. I've had my eye on her."

"Since when were you on the B-girl detail?"

"She's done other things. Loads of other things."

The plainclothesman looked uncertain.

"I said I'd take care of it," said Sanducci, and shoved Allie into the sedan. When he got in beside her, he was chuckling. "I told you not to try it," he said.

"You rigged that?"

"How could I rig it? But if he hadn't picked you up, I was going to. Now maybe you'll behave."

"Maybe."

They drove in silence. Allie didn't notice where they went. Sanducci glanced at her from time to time.

"Breathing heavily isn't going to do you any good," he said at last. He sounded real relaxed. It made her so mad. "I could turn you back to that guy. I could turn you in myself. He don't like tarts. He treats them real mean."

"I'm no tart."

"Opinions differ. Anyway, you're going to be. You know what that guy likes to do? I think he's peculiar or something. Maybe his mother brought him up wrong. He likes to pull in punks and kids like you, and you know what he does? He turns a cold hose on them. It doesn't sound like much, I know. But he does it by the hour. It drives them crazy. He's got a good record. He's Irish. Nobody pays any attention." He glanced at her.

Allie had had her hand on the door.

"No, don't try that. It wouldn't do you any good. You behave, see?"

"I see." Allie knew when she was licked.

"It won't be so bad. After all, you like it," he said.

"What do you want me to do?"

"Me? I don't want you to do anything. But it so happens I have a friend. You've met her. She hangs out at the Jickey. She's young but she's enterprising. She sort of helps out a Chinese merchant now and then. You like the Chinese? She specializes. You don't like that? Well, she's got another friend. A couple. They feel sorry for people. A tired businessman wants to go for a weekend, and the way they figure it, why should he go alone? Maybe he doesn't go away. But he says three days, you stay three days, see? You get a hundred bucks."

Allie's eyes widened.

"Only they pay it to me. I keep seventy. That way you don't run any expenses. This thirty I bank. That's so you don't run away. Then if you're good, well, I'm honest. I understand how things are. A month or two, you behave yourself, maybe you get the cash."

Allie was fit to be tied.

"You hear me?" demanded Sanducci.

"I hear you."

Sanducci chuckled. "That's right," he said. "A little practice and you'll get so you read good." He leaned over and patted her knee. His hands were dry and tough. "And that punk Purvis would've given you two bits and you'd have been glad to get it. The nerve of him. I taught him all he knows. Then he turns on me and tries to show me up, over a cheap bill of goods like you. You should have it so good."

He felt pretty good himself. Vera was right about him. He'd had it easy so long he'd gotten soft. He thought he was safe. Torrey he'd dismissed as harmless. He hadn't a worry in the world, and the sort of clients he had, Allie would go down big, and a buck was a buck.

There he was wrong. Torrey wasn't harmless. Torrey was all ready to move in on one of his side shows, and drive him into the open that way.

He was going to begin with Pop.

Sanducci had forgotten all about Pop. To him Pop was just a sucker who was all nailed down and paid up regular.

CHAPTER SIXTEEN

JANEY stayed in her room. Seven-fifty wouldn't take her far. If she stayed in her room, maybe they'd leave her alone about the rent. Besides, she was afraid to go out. In her room at least she was safe. She had her food sent in from a Chinese kitchen and waited for Allie to come back. She didn't quite know why, but Allie was the only person she knew, and she needed help.

But this time it was Allie who didn't come back.

After three days of waiting round for her, Janey was desperate. She jumped at every sound. What can a girl do when she only has two dollars left? She was sure Allie had abandoned her. Allie had tricked her into coming to San Francisco in the first place. Why shouldn't Allie trick her again? She felt bitter. She knew now Allie was no friend. Allie only used people and then waltzed on in search of somebody else. All Allie wanted was a good time.

All the same Janey needed someone at least to talk to. When a tap comes on your door after three days, you jump up to answer it. That is what she did. She was all ready to tell Allie she didn't mind. That she had been worried about her. That she wondered where she had been.

She didn't get the chance. It wasn't Allie standing out there. It was Purvis and Pedersen.

"Oh," she said, and backed into the room. Purvis and Pedersen walked right in, and looked round contemptuously. There was a milk carton on the dresser and French fries from hamburgers in the wastepaper basket. They summed that situation up, and she didn't blame them. It was sordid.

"We thought maybe you could use a little cash," said Purvis, in that furry voice of his. Pedersen stuck his thumbs into his belt loops. "Yeah," he echoed. "You made a big hit with Pop."

They stood watching her for a minute, while Pedersen rocked back and forth on his heels. They had horseshoe plates on them that stuck out around the edge. She knew why Purvis brought him along. But it wasn't necessary. Something in her had given up for a while. She was passive. And what difference did it make whether there was one set of stills or fifty? She had to eat.

"Now?" she asked.

Purvis held her coat for her with mock gallantry. "Now," he said. There was a sort of mean twinkle in his eye, but he looked at her curiously. Maybe he had expected her to put up a fight. Certainly Pedersen would have liked that. But she was too worn-out to fight.

They went out through the lobby. The clerk stopped them. He wanted his rent again. Purvis stepped up and paid it. He was sort of grand about it, in a small-time way.

"You see how easy it is if you string along?" he said, when he joined them in the car. He was amused about something. She didn't want to know what. They drove in silence until they reached the alley. She sat between them. They wanted it that way, just in case.

"You know," drawled Purvis, "I just can't figure her out."

"She's small town," said Pedersen. "With small town types it takes longer."

"A farm girl, you mean, would be different?"

"Yeah," agreed Pedersen. "You never been on a farm, honey?"

Janey shook her head and stared in front of her.

"Well, we all have to learn sometime," said Purvis, and pulled up the car. Still on either side of her, they shepherded her into the back of the building and down to the basement. This time they locked the stair door behind them. Janey scarcely noticed.

She was too embarrassed. But if it was only like last time, she wouldn't mind too much.

Still, subconsciously she heard the click, and subconsciously it must have disturbed her. Something was not quite the way it had been last time.

Pop was nervous. He was at the far end of the basement again, which was now disguised with a flat covered with bedroom wallpaper. There was also a bed, surrounded by reflectors, which still left room for artistic deep shadows. Pop was at the cameras, talking to a thin, jumpy man with blinking eyes. He was a parody of a handsome stranger. He had black hair and a small moustache, but his cheeks were sallow and his mouth was over-ripe. He was wearing a dirty terrycloth robe with a monogram and he was smoking a cigarette. The robe was blue. So were his pajamas. He was jerky. He looked as though he took dope.

Purvis said "hello" to him. The man looked pained.

"I don't like the feel of today," said Pop. "I got the feeling that something is going to happen. It just feels all wrong."

"Nothing's going to happen, Pop."

"Somebody phoned me last night. He said maybe I should lie low today."

"I'll go get you an astrologer, and he'll tell you anything you want to hear," said Purvis.

"Does the girl know what she has to do?"

Purvis grinned. So did Pedersen. "Hell no. You want this authentic, don't you?"

Janey didn't know what they were talking about. She looked at them blankly. The man in the bathrobe looked at her with disgust and then shrugged. His face had the jerky, vacant, foolish expression of a porcelain doll. He glanced at Purvis and Pedersen.

"You don't know us," said Pedersen. "You never did and you don't now. Come on, let's get on with it. We haven't got all day."

Pop was loading the magazine of the film camera. It was the sort used for home movies, but more complicated in the lens. He swore.

"You should have told her," he said. "I don't want no trouble." He looked apprehensively towards the ceiling.

"You're protected, aren't you?"

"Sure. I give Sanducci two hundred a month. But how do I know who has something on him?"

"Shut up," snaped Purvis. He turned to Janey. "Well, what are you waiting for? You want a dressing room or something?"

Janey woke up and went to change miserably behind a packing case. She tried to hide herself, as she got into the negligee. She looked up and Pedersen was watching her. She blushed.

She came out uncertainly, and stood in front of the camera.

"I thought we were having stills," she said.

Purvis laughed, even though his face looked narrow and eager. "Pay her in advance, Pop. Let's see what she does for money."

Pop hesitated.

"I said pay her."

Pop counted out fifty bucks. Purvis reached for it. But Pedersen got it first. "No," he said. "Let her have all of it."

"Since when did you get so soft?" demanded Purvis.

"Hell, she's just a kid."

Janey looked from one to the other. Purvis backed down; He didn't like it, but he decided to let it go. "That's better," said Pedersen. "There's no reason why you should get paid for your thrills all the time." He shoved the money awkwardly at Janey. "Here. Take it." He sounded gravelly and angry. "I said take it."

She took it and shoved it into her bra. Pop noticed the bra under the negligee. "Okay," he said. "Maybe it's better that way."

The guy in the bathrobe stepped out of camera range. Janey sat down and tried to pretend it wasn't happening again. Pedersen swore and then chinned himself on a waterpipe running along the ceiling.

"Okay," shouted Pop and started the camera.

They all bent forward intently.

Janey shut her eyes and leaned back on the bed. She was confused. She had expected Pedersen. She looked up and saw the man in the bathrobe film. Everyone was very still. She could only hear the sound of Pop's breathing and her own.

There were sounds of heavy footsteps overhead. Just at that moment Janey realized what kind of movie this was. She clenched her teeth and shook. A hot and cold wave of shame and fear swept over her. The man in the bathrobe halted. He looked up, too. They all did.

"Jesus," said Pop. "It's a raid."

"Don't get overexcited Pop."

Someone was hammering on the cellar door. The man in the bathrobe made a dive for a packing case. He went so fast he wasn't missed.

"My camera," said Pop. "Everything. That desk. What's going to happen?"

"To hell with your camera. How do we get out of here?"

Someone was beating against the door. It wouldn't hold long. The cops didn't bother to ask them to open up.

Pop danced up and down. The camera ground on.

"Smash it," shouted Purvis. He picked up a spare tripod and brought it down on the camera. The camera fell on the floor, still grinding. Pedersen understood. He kicked the film case, until it came away. Once it was light exposed it couldn't be used as evidence.

Pop wrung his hands and then made a bee-line for the back of the set, ripping it away. Behind was another room. "The street lift," he shouted. The room was under the sidewalk. The light was there, with its loop to push up the iron doors above. He jumped on and started it. Janey ran after Purvis and Pedersen. The lift was already going up. Purvis and Pedersen scrambled for it. Janey didn't stop to think. She ran for it too. Behind them they heard the door crash open and steps rushing down the cellar.

"You tipped somebody off," shouted Purvis.

"She can't come dressed like that," snapped Pop. The iron loop above the lift touched the doors. They began to rise.

Purvis shoved her off. The lift was now about five feet off the ground. She fell on her back, on the concrete floor, and sobbing, crawled away. There was no place to hide. None of the junk in there was large enough. The lift flung back the gates. Purvis, Pedersen, and Pop leaped off.

Janey turned, shaking, and faced the door.

She could hear voices in the main cellar now. They must have caught the man in the bathrobe. She heard him screaming like a rabbit. They could hear the cops talking. They had found the camera.

"No evidence." She heard it flung aside.

"Maybe junior here would talk, if we took him off his dope."

"They'd have him sprung by then."

"Take him in anyway."

Footsteps came closer. Janey shrank back, trying to hide herself, but there wasn't any place to hide. She looked towards the door, and then gasped. It was Torrey.

He stood there. He was surprised all right, but not much. After all the Tenderloin was a small place. He knew he'd run into her somewhere. It was a circular track that was hard to get out of. But he hadn't expected to find her in a place like this. If she was at all the way he thought she was, that didn't figure.

But he did know whose side he was on. He was on her side. It was so natural he wasn't even surprised about it. His mind worked fast. "There's nobody in here," he called over his shoulder. "They got out through the lift to the street. We might catch 'em if we're quick."

It was his raid. Nobody questioned that.

"Upstairs," he snapped. He turned round and went out.

Janey heard them moving away up the stairs. Suddenly it was very quiet. There was an empty carton against the wall. She sank down on it. Her hands were bleeding, from her fall. Maybe half an hour went by.

Then she heard a noise. She waited. The footsteps came nearer. It was Torrey. She didn't know what to say to him. She just stared. Her jaw was trembling.

Suddenly he smiled. "Come on," he said. "It isn't as bad as that. Get dressed."

She didn't answer.

He shoved his cap to the back of his head. "Don't worry," he said. "I won't even ask you how you got in this one." He looked at her more closely. "Come on." He was very gentle. "What's your name?"

"Janey."

"I'm Torrey. Come on. Your clothes must be here somewhere. You'll have to hurry. I haven't got much time."

He came forward and raised her up. She moved into the other room in a sort of dream. She put on her clothes.

He glanced the other way while she did it. Somehow he felt shy. "Hurry," he said. "The others may be back. We can talk later."

She crouched down and got dressed. "That's better," he said. "We'll go out the back way." He took her arm.

"Why are you doing this?"

His face changed expression. "I don't know," he said. "Maybe you look lost or something. But I don't think that's it. Put it down as a good deed."

"I am lost."

"Nothing's as bad as that." He looked at his watch as they went up the stairs. He had already decided to see her later. "Can you get home all right?"

She nodded.

"Where's home?"

"*The Florida.*"

He frowned. "How did you get in that flea-trap?"

"Allie picked it."

"Have they got something on you?"

"Who?"

"Purvis and Pedersen. It was them wasn't it?"

She nodded. She half-smiled, despite herself. And it was the half smile that did it as far as he was concerned. "They think you and I are friends. Because of the theatre and Sanducci."

He was suddenly cautious. "What's he got to do with it?"

"They think Allie and I are stool pigeons or something."

"Where's Allie? She's your girl friend, isn't she? The blonde?"

"I don't know."

Torrey looked up and down the street. "Go back and lock your door. Don't open it for anybody. Even Allie. I'll knock four times and then once. I'll come as soon as I can."

He knew he would, too. He was even beginning to know why.

She turned and walked down the street, and he looked after her. But when she turned around at the corner, he wasn't there. She went back to the hotel.

CHAPTER SEVENTEEN

O F ALL THE DAMN FOOL THINGS Allie kept a diary. No one had ever seen it but Janey. Well, she had a lot to put in it now. Probably nobody ever knows what sets girls like Allie off, but once they get started, they keep on going until they run down or smash up. They aren't bad. They aren't good. They just don't have any moral sense at all. Most people have a conscience. The only time Allie was plagued by conscience was when she wasn't getting what she wanted. She always blamed herself for that. It was her fault for not knowing how.

She wasn't even tough about it. She was all peaches and cream. She was just shrewd. And now she was over the tough bit. All she had to do now was to get on a good circuit, so she met enough guys, and then figure out how to drop Sanducci. She just hated to see all that money go into his pocket instead of into hers.

That first guy Sanducci got for her really opened her eyes. Now she knew what she could get. She'd never met a rich man before. She'd never even met a man who made a good living. She hadn't realized how easy it was to get things out of them. She began to dream about clothes, and jewelry, and loads of good food. That's what she went to the movies to see, and now she saw that that was what she could get.

Once, in cinemascope, she'd seen a waiter serve lobster and the lobster had slid forward until it had filled the whole screen, bright red and knobby. It wasn't the lobster that got her. It was the cracked ice. Sam, that was the guy's name, had taken her to some restaurant in North Beach. He had thought it was funny.

She didn't care what he thought. There she was having lobster in cracked ice.

The trouble was, Monday morning there was Sanducci waiting for her, when she left Sam's apartment. He hadn't any business in a ritzy district like that. It was on one of the hills. But Sanducci wasn't taking any chances.

He held the door open for her and she got in.

"How'd it go?"

"It was all right," she said. She didn't want to tell him anything. But she didn't have to. He just chuckled. Then he paid her off. That is, he gave her a little spending money. Anyone would think he was doing her a favor, or something.

"You know," he said, "you and me might get along after all."

She didn't answer. She watched traffic.

"Only if you get any ideas," he said sharply, "you let me know first."

She shrugged.

He dropped her off at *The Florida*. *The Florida* looked drippy to her now. Now she'd seen something else. She wrinkled her nose, and he didn't miss that either.

"I'll be round tonight or tomorrow," he said. "You get a rest. You might need it."

"Don't you know when?"

"I got worries of my own. You needn't worry. I'll be round."

She looked up and down the street, glad he was in plain clothes. The neighborhood reminded her of Purvis and Pedersen, and she didn't want to tangle with them again, except maybe to pay them back. And maybe to show off a little in front of Purvis. Purvis was small time and she wanted to show him she knew it.

She went up to her room. Janey was out. That pleased Allie just as well. She sat down and hauled out her diary and began to write it up. She had her own code. She made little asterisks if she'd had a good time, and now she put three rows of double asterisks against the three days she'd been gone. It kept her happy. She wrote slowly, in a big sloppy hand.

Then she went out to get a snack. When she came back it was dusk. There was a light under Janey's door, but Allie went right on to her own room. But later, when she heard four knocks and then another on Janey's door she was curious. And when she heard voices in the next room she went over to the door in her stocking feet, to listen.

And what she heard really rocked her back on her heels. She didn't think Janey had it in her.

CHAPTER EIGHTEEN

JANEY felt something in her she hadn't felt before, and didn't dare to trust it. It was excitement. It was something she had never felt about any man before, or any boy, for that matter, and so she couldn't quite know what it was that she felt. She only knew that she was restless, and not nearly so ashamed or frightened as she felt she should be. She had no idea how he felt about the matter. Probably he only felt sorry for her, because she was a fool. Or maybe he was just after her. That is what Allie would have said. But somehow she didn't think so. He wasn't the sort of man Allie knew all about, somehow she sensed that. She thought he was good.

She had a bath and dressed. She dressed with particular care. She didn't even realize she was doing it. After all, there was no reason for him to come, unless he wanted something. Yet she knew he would come. She felt strangely calm. She had the feeling that now everything would be all right. It was silly. She'd only seen him once before to speak to.

When she heard his knock on the door she jumped convulsively. It was dark, but she hadn't even bothered to turn the lights on, except for the one by the bed. Now she flicked on the switch, smoothed down her skirt, and let him in.

He was in plainclothes, a fawn sports jacket, a black shirt open at the neck, and fawn slacks. She was overwhelmed. He was like those boys at the high school in Manteca she always looked up to and never met, the ones Allie had never met either, the proper ones. The ones with style, not gaudy style, but real style.

She'd never opened the door on anyone like that in her life. It was wonderful. But there was something else about him too, something she instantly understood and trusted.

"Ask me in," he said. He was smiling.

"Oh yes. Of course." She stepped back into the room and then closed the door after him. She was fussed. She was ashamed of the room. It never occurred to her that he might take her as she was.

They stood facing each other. They either had to embrace or talk. The emotion between them was like that. Instead he wandered restlessly round the room. After all, he scarcely knew why he had come himself.

"I guess you think this is pretty odd," he said.

She glanced at him and then shook her head.

He sat down on the edge of the bed. It was the only place to sit. "Well, I think it is," he said. "I've never done anything like this in my life."

She misunderstood him. She wondered hopelessly if he'd just come the way men came to Allie. She wouldn't blame him. But something inside her almost died at the thought of it.

He looked up and caught her thought. And it made him angry. She could see it did.

"Oh hell, that's not what I mean," he said. "Do I look like someone like that?"

She shook her head. He looked up at her again. "It isn't going so well, is it?" he asked. He cocked his head on one side. "I could go out and come in again. That would mean I'd been here before and we were old friends."

Despite herself she smiled.

"That's better," he said. "That's much better. About this morning. We could forget that if you like. We could pretend it didn't happen. I said I wouldn't ask you any questions. Maybe I should have brought flowers or a box of chocolate. I could go out and get some. I'm not very good at this."

She half smiled again. "No," she said, "you're not.

"Well, I meant to be nice."

"Oh you are," she said. Despite herself, abruptly, she sat down on the bed and began to cry. The tears blotted him out. It was silly, but she couldn't help it.

Suddenly he was sitting beside her and had his arms around her. His coat smelled tweedy and damp. She buried her head in it, but tried to hold herself together. He stroked her hair.

"You shouldn't do that," she sobbed.

He knew he shouldn't do that. If they were caught together, he'd be ruined. Some people were longing to get something on him. But somehow just at the moment he didn't care. He'd just wanted to be nice. But now he found he liked her better than he thought.

He held her more tightly. She needed to be held. He could feel that through the thin stuff of her dress. Somehow it was settled between them. Now she had someone to talk to.

"Oh where's Allie," she said.

"Who's Allie?" He was bewildered.

"She was the one who got me here."

"Oh, the girl you were with." He hesitated. "How *did* she get you here?"

"I can't tell you."

"It might be better for you if you did."

She sat up straight, clenched her knuckles, and stared at him. It was as though she felt that he thought so little of her that he might as well think even less. She turned her face slightly away. He was touched. It would be better for her to get it out of her system. Then they could go on from there.

So she told him about it. She had been crossing a field, on the way back from seeing Allie. It was summer and school was out. One of the field laborers had raped her. She didn't even know his name, except that it was Chris or something. She didn't know much about such things. She thought she was pregnant. She was ashamed to go to a doctor. She lived with her aunt, and if she had known, her aunt would have flung her out. Her aunt was like that. So she had told Allie. And Allie had persuaded her to run away to San Francisco, to earn enough money to have the thing taken care of.

"And I wasn't," said Janey. "She knew all along I wasn't. So here I am and I can't go back. She told everybody. And now all this has happened."

"All what?" he asked softly.

She didn't know all of it. She didn't know what Allie had done to Sparkman, and she didn't know the arrangement between Allie and Sanducci. But she did know about the rest of it. She knew about Vera, and Purvis, and Pedersen, Pop, the guy with the funny movies, and the gang at the Jickey Club. Torrey began to fit the pieces together. His job was to get Sanducci. He saw she might be of help. It didn't occur to him yet that something might be going on that even Sanducci didn't know about.

"If I back you up, will you tell about all this?" he asked. "I mean, perhaps in Court?"

She looked up at him, scared, and then slowly nodded. "If you want me to," she said. She sounded discouraged.

"That isn't why I came," he told her. "Really."

"Oh you shouldn't say things like that," she said. "Not after all you know about me. Look where you found me."

"I might not have found you at all, otherwise."

"But it's all so dirty," she said. "And I'm in with them now. They'll use me against you. I don't know how, but they will. They'll trick you. They'll pull you down, too."

He knew then how much she liked him. No one had ever liked him quite that way before.

"You aren't pulled down," he told her. "You just have to hang on until we can get you out, that's all."

"But why are you helping me?" she asked. She looked at him unbelievingly.

"I don't know. Because I want to."

"But that's crazy."

He wasn't holding onto her now. They were sitting side by side. He clasped his hands between his legs and stared down at the dreary pattern of the rug. "No," he said slowly, "I don't think it is. Sometimes you just meet somebody, that's all."

"Oh."

He looked up sharply. "What?"

"Nothing. It's just that you always looked so nice. Even there at the bus station, when we first came." Her voice trailed away. But she couldn't help noticing him. He was the sort of person she had always wanted to meet. And she had met him in the wrong place, and besides, she was only a girl. She was too young for him.

She looked round the room. She saw it in all its horrible detail. She saw the scratches on the dresser, and the brokendown mirror, the bed creaked under them, and it was a slut's room. She didn't even want to be seen in it. It made her feel unclean. The silence lengthened out. He must have noticed what she was thinking.

"I came to take you to dinner," he said. "You need to get out of here."

She shrank from being seen in public. "I couldn't," she said.

He stood up and went to the closet. He came back with a coat, and held it out for her.

"Not that one," she said. "The other one."

They looked at each other blankly, and then began to laugh.

"There," he said. His voice was gruff and warm. "You see, you feel better. Once a woman starts worrying about her clothes, she feels better." He went to the closet and got her the other coat, and held it while she slipped into it. He pressed her waist slightly with his hands, and then let her go.

"Come on," he said, "we'll have fun." He held the door open for her, closed it after her, locked it, and gave her the key. Neither of them looked back.

That was just as well. Allie was at her keyhole, watching them go down the corridor. At first she had thought it funny, a timid mouse like Janey snagging a handsome cop. She thought it went to prove her own ideas about human nature. But when Janey had spilled the beans that way, it scared her. Things were hard enough, what with Sanducci and the gang at the Jickey Club, without Janey making it worse. She knew if Janey tipped off a cop, she, Allie, would get the blame. And that would mean that Sanducci would have her where he wanted her even more than he did now, for she'd need him for protection. She was all ready to tear after them, she didn't know why, and try to stop Janey from spilling anything else. Janey was a fool. But she didn't dare leave the room. She had to wait for Sanducci, or else get it in the neck.

She watched them go down the corridor with something like fury. Torrey was the kind of man she never got. That was why she wanted all the others, just to get even with the stuck-up prigs who wouldn't have her. Allie wanted to show everybody. And uneasily, at the back of her mind, she sensed that that was why she did what she did.

She came to a boil. Just as everything looked as though it were going okay, Janey suddenly upped and overturned the whole damn thing. That was how she thought she thought about it. But just for a minute there she was uncertain. She was uneasy. She couldn't get over the idea that Janey would want to get something on her, out of revenge. That is what she would have done, and so she thought that was what Janey would do, now that she had a policeman, too.

She sat down to wait for Sanducci.

CHAPTER NINETEEN

TORREY was watching Janey. It gave him a lot of pleasure. He didn't know now why he had gone to see her. He did know he was liking her better and better as the evening went on.

He'd stopped pretending he'd rescued her from the cellar on the off-chance she might turn evidence against Sanducci's suckers. It would be nice if she would, but that wasn't why he'd gotten her out of there. And it wasn't the real reason he was seeing her, either. Also he knew he was going to see more of her. He just had to. There was something about her that got him.

She was only a girl, but she had something he had always been looking for, and never found. Maybe it was a strange kind of stubborn courage. She'd had it that first day he spotted her at the station. Probably that's why he'd remembered her.

He had gotten her right away from the whole sordid district. He had taken her to the other side of town. Janey had never had such a time. It made her sparkle. She unfolded. She became beautiful and touching. He knew what was happening, all right. He was beginning to fall in love with her. He'd always avoided getting mixed up with someone, but now he didn't care a bit. It might be awkward, he could see that, but that didn't matter. Watching her was fun.

She had the ability to be delighted with things. When she was pleased her whole face lit up with a wonderful smile that made it a pleasure to please her. Instinctively she liked things just so. It was just that she'd never had them.

He took her to a good restaurant. Then he took her dancing, to a quiet, placid place with dreamy music and the right dim lights. He had only wanted to be kind. He found that he had never enjoyed himself so much before.

Neither had Janey. She wished the evening would never end. It was like Cinderella, only worse. And she watched him, too. She got him to talk about himself.

He told her everything except the immediate nature of his job. He didn't dare do that. He came from Colma. He was a career policeman. This was his break. He was unmarried and lonely. He was a little puzzled about life and a little wistful. He was a man who kept to himself. Now he opened up.

Janey might have been naïve by Allie's standards, but she was grown-up in other ways. She realized suddenly that he was lonely, too, and that made them more together. When he took her hand, it seemed the most natural thing in the world, and she returned the pressure quickly. It was as though their feeling for each other was a secret they had to keep, even from themselves. Something in her was old enough to realize that instinctively. But it made her very happy. She knew she had found someone she would see again, and that made all the difference in the world.

By the time they had to go back to the hotel, it was almost as though they were engaged. Somehow they knew each other, and had known each other for a long time.

He saw her up to her room. She thought wryly that that was the advantage of a hotel like that. She didn't even flinch when the desk clerk gave her a wise look. For now she knew what he couldn't: that no matter what he might think, this was different.

She unlocked her door, and he stepped inside. She didn't feel so badly about that awful room now.

He looked at her for a moment, and then he embraced her and kissed her goodnight. She held on to him for a long time. He didn't really want to go. She didn't really want him to go. But she wasn't Allie, and he wasn't that kind of man.

"Will you be all right" he asked.

Her eyes were still shiny. She nodded.

Hastily he scribbled something on a slip of paper. "You can usually get me here," he said. "Or they'll know where to find me. It's the police station, but don't let that bother you. The other number's my apartment." He hesitated, embarrassed. "Do you have any money?"

She said she had. She had the money from that morning, at Pop's, the money Pedersen had gotten her. That seemed very far away.

"Don't tell anybody about us," he said. "I'm sorry, but by now you know why." She scarcely heard him. "It won't be long."

Then he shrugged. He smiled at her half comically. He couldn't stay any longer, and they were both sorry. He went out and closed the door gently behind him.

But not so gently that Allie didn't hear it. Allie had a hall-bedroom instinct about these things. For a moment they had sat on the bed again, the springs had creaked, and from that Allie had gotten her own ideas.

So she thought she had a weapon over Janey now, if she needed to use it. That made her feel better, for Sanducci hadn't turned up, and knowing Torrey was after Sanducci might be useful soon. For she had the feeling things were going on she didn't know about, as though a web were tightening around her. She wanted protection against that.

CHAPTER TWENTY

S HE WAS RIGHT about the web tightening around her. It was.
But protection wasn't going to help. For one thing there were
too many people to be protected against.

Vera, Purvis and Pedersen had made their getaway, and
taken Pop with them. Pop was shaking like a leaf. They had a
hideaway for emergencies like that, a hideaway so public, and yet
so secret, that it was almost foolproof. They dumped him there
and told him to keep his mouth shut. He had his own place, of
course, but the way things were going, he might need that one
later. Besides, Pop wasn't dependable really. He was the kind who
might blab to save his own skin. They left him a bottle of whisky.
If he got swacked he wouldn't be able to run away, and a bottle of
whisky usually laid him out flat.

Then they held a council of war.

The problem was, who had tipped the police off? And they
were beginning to be nervous. They almost had a falling out
about that.

Purvis wandered round the room, biting his nails. Vera
watched him contemptuously. He didn't like that. Vera made him
nervous. She was the only one there who really had the drop on
him. He looked at his chewed up nails and began to sing under
his breath. He closed his eyes. He disappeared into the song. He
forgot she was there.

It seemed to him that things had gotten a little out of hand,
and he blamed Vera. Vera was always up to tricks. You never
knew where you stood with her. It was Vera who had forced

him into the big time, if you could call what they were doing the big time. Of course she split with them. He had loads of clothes and money in the bank. They all had. But where she kept her money was a mystery, and stealing cars had been a lot safer. She was the one who had found Pop and his dirty pictures. Well that was all right, for Pedersen was the one who took the risk there. And Pedersen hated Vera. Purvis couldn't figure that out.

The prostitution was all right too. Sanducci covered them there. But what they were doing now was another matter. Dope was bad, and Sanducci didn't even know about the dope. He'd be scared of dope, and with the Vice Squad closing in, he'd turn them in on that as soon as he got the chance, if he found out about it. Dope was real trouble, and Sanducci was small stuff. Maybe they all were.

Vera told him to shut up. "You'll be taking the stuff yourself if you go on that way," she said.

Pedersen was the only one of them who was at ease. He lolled over a packing case, with his head on the floor and his boots propped up in Vera's face, as usual. Being insolent with Vera was one of his amusements.

"You know, baby, you're acting real peculiar these days," he said.

"What do you mean by that?"

"That's what I mean by that." His swung his feet apart and stared at her. "You wouldn't be planning to act up on us would you?"

"You're crazy?"

"I was just wondering. You must have quite a nest egg by now."

"You haven't done so badly," she snapped.

He grinned. "Neither have you. Where'd you run to, if you thought maybe you could run?"

"Nobody's running."

"Probably you'd throw the police a fish first. Who would it be? Me? Purvis? Who?"

"I said you're crazy."

He swung to his feet. "No, I'm not crazy. I just wouldn't like to see you try it, that's all. It might be unhealthy."

Vera glowered at him.

"One of us gets it, we all get it," he said. "Where does the dope come from anyhow?"

"We get it. Pop receives it. And there's the boat."

"Pop isn't going to receive it no more. So you set up another fall guy. That's all that worries me. Or did you tip Sanducci off?"

"Sanducci doesn't have anything to do with this. You know that."

Pedersen jumped to his feet and hauled out his knife. "Yeah, so you say. But how do we know?"

Vera wasn't scared of him, but she didn't say anything. Purvis had stopped singing. He looked puzzled and a little scared. "Ah Ed," he said. "That stuff won't get you anywhere with Vera."

"What does?" demanded Pedersen, and sat down again. "Just the same, if she hadn't brought that dumb brunette into Pop's we might have been right where we were."

"She didn't have anything to do with it," snapped Vera.

"How do you know?" demanded Purvis. "You thought she was a stool yourself. For that guy Torrey. Why don't he and Sanducci get on better? Maybe you should tell them to synchronize."

Pedersen was tired of it. "Sparkman," he said.

They both turned to him.

He shrugged. "Well, who picked them up, except for Purvis with Allie here, and that didn't get far."

Purvis chopped his arms down at his side. "She wasn't worth having. She wouldn't work."

"Not for you maybe. But she worked for Sparkman. It was even a real job. Who picked her up when I wanted to get to her in the first place? Sparkman. And who's in thick with Sanducci?

Sparkman. Who got us dealing with hopheads? Sparkman. And what do you do about him? When he gets dribbly he'd tell anybody anything. Suppose Allie is a stool pigeon? Just think what she's got on us."

For Pedersen it was a long speech.

"Hell, a week ago we didn't even know she was alive. Or that girl friend of hers either."

"You know it now though," said Pedersen.

Purvis and Vera looked at each other. Then they turned to Pedersen.

"Okay, where is he?"

"How should I know?"

"You mean he's disappeared?"

"Or lying low. Or in police custody. Take your pick."

"We've got to find him." said Vera abruptly.

"Sure. Where do we start?" asked Pedersen.

"He's got an apartment somewhere, hasn't he?"

"Sure, he's got an apartment. Are you sure Janey wouldn't be a better bet, though?" He watched her narrowly.

"You stop that. We haven't got any time to lose."

"You working on a time schedule or something?"

"It isn't a good idea to needle me," said Vera. "What's that girl to you, anyhow?"

"I just like her. Does that bother you, sweetheart? If so I'll go right ahead with it."

Vera spat and headed for the door. They made sure Pop was bedded down, and then drove over to Sparkman's motel. His apartment was still a shambles, but he'd gotten out under his own steam, and the caretaker didn't know a thing. All told, it took them two days to find him.

He was in a hospital out in the Mission district, a great big Norman style building rearing out of dirty slums and shaded by trees clogged with soot. Going up the steps they made a curious group, Vera like a miniature woman, with a tight, angry face, Purvis with his sideburns, wiping his nose nervously, and Pedersen clopping along in his leather jacket and boots. The receptionist looked them over without favor, but it wasn't any of her business. They were sent on up.

Sparkman was in a semi-private room on the third floor. He had three broken ribs, skin lacerations, and a skull concussion. The funny thing was that once his head began to clear he liked the way the ribs hurt when he breathed. He would take a series of rapid breaths, wince, and then giggle. He was such a flabby man that he sort of oozed over the sheets. When they came in he was propped up on two pillows, reading a copy of the *Reader's Digest*. Someone had brought him a pile of sadistic comics, too. These were stacked in a neat pile beside his medicines. But he looked old and fallen apart. He looked very old indeed.

Pedersen leaned against the wall next to the door. Purvis went to the window. It was an ominous arrangement. Vera stood at the foot of the bed. His eyes flickered from one to the other of them.

"How did you find out I was here?" he demanded. "You didn't phone my wife, did you?"

"We went down the hospital list. Also the morgue, but you weren't there yet," said Vera. "They said you'd be in later."

Sparkman looked relieved. But not much. "What do you want?"

"They're closing in on us, in case you hadn't heard," said Pedersen. "They got Pop yesterday. We think maybe the girls might have something to do with it. Or you."

"What girls?"

"You know what girls. Those little darlings you got jobs for."

Sparkman apparently gave up on Pedersen. Pedersen was a little too real for comfort. He looked at Vera instead.

"Keep your voice down, for Pete's sake," said Vera. There was a cloth screen between the two beds in the room, but that didn't keep out sound, and everybody in a hospital listens to everybody else.

Sparkman looked scared.

"Well," she said. "Cough up. Where's the blonde, that girl Allie or whatever her name is."

Sparkman looked evasive.

"You want me to take your comic books away?" asked Vera. "We went to your hangout. What happened?"

"She beat me up."

"I don't want to know your sex life. What happened?"

"Sanducci came in. He took her away."

"Just like that?"

"She took my camera."

"Oh to hell with your camera," said Vera. For the first time in all this she really looked upset. "What did he want her for?"

Sparkman shrugged.

"You didn't tell her anything, did you?"

"What about?"

"You know what about. How we get shipments, and that kind of thing."

"Sanducci wouldn't try a double cross," said Purvis.

"How the hell would you know?" snapped Vera. She turned to Sparkman again. "Where did he take her?"

Sparkman just shook his head.

Vera stepped closer to the bed.

"Aw, hell, honey, he don't know," said Purvis. "You don't want to go making a scene now."

Vera turned to Pedersen, but Pedersen was on Purvis' side again. "He's right," he said. "Let's get going." But his eyes were darkly alive. He was a watcher. He looked at people and didn't say anything. But when a watcher starts to put two and two together, anything is apt to happen. Vera did as she was told.

"Hey," yelled Sparkman. "What's going to happen to me?"

"Little man," said Purvis over his shoulder, "you don't even count."

"You know what I mean," said Sparkman. "Sanducci got me in with you."

It was Vera's turn to stop. "You needed the money, didn't you?" she said. "You shut up. And that means with Sanducci, too."

Sparkman shut up.

They went down the corridor and out into the daylight. Purvis felt better now. He put on his dark glasses. They gave him a sense of privacy. Behind them he could really feel as though he was running the whole bunch of them. He teetered back and forth on his toes. "Okay," he said, "where now?"

Pedersen shrugged. "Go to the hotel and pick up the girl."

"That might not be so easy."

"What about the other one. The one Sanducci's sidekick seems to like."

"He isn't any sidekick of Sanducci's," said Vera. She always stuck up for him when things got too tight. It was hard to see why. "Sanducci's got troubles of his own."

CHAPTER TWENTY-ONE

HAT WAS JUST EXACTLY what Sanducci was beginning to find out, and it made him sweat blood. Sanducci might have been a big man to Purvis and the gang, but he was a little man everywhere else. For ten years he'd been able to take his graft, and nobody said a word. Now it looked as though he was being shaped up for fall guy. Not that anyone said anything to him directly, but the boys down at headquarters were beginning to avoid him, and he knew what that meant.

A cop who makes money on the side has troubles of his own. Protection money is one thing. But Sanducci had been enterprising. He'd moved on to better things. He had the call-girl setup. Pop was one of his sidelines. He'd helped finance Pop. And then there was Sparkman. A little blackmail and a few threats, and Sparkman had made all sorts of contacts possible. Sparkman wasn't interested in that kind of thing himself. Like most fetishists and such like, Sparkman liked what he liked and nothing else. But once Sanducci had gotten things set up, the money had started to roll in. And on a cop's salary, that had been hard to hide. He couldn't pretend someone had left him a legacy. He couldn't leave it in the bank, because the State checked and taxed all deposits over a certain sum. He had to keep it in motion, on the stock-market, and under assumed names, and when it was in cash, he had to stash it away. Vera had been a big help that way. Even so there were a lot of things he hadn't told even her.

And once in a while you met somebody who couldn't be paid off. That was what had happened now. Then there was the devil to pay. After all, he couldn't very well clear out, and he was too well known to lie low. All he could do was cover up.

Whoever was on his tail, was being smart about it, like that raid on Pop's. And Torrey had led that raid. It might have been a coincidence, but somehow Sanducci didn't think so. Usually they paired him off with somebody he knew. Where Torrey had come from, he didn't even know, and Torrey wasn't crooked, at least Sanducci didn't think so. And he was damned if he was going to lose everything, just because a couple of dumb girls from some hick town, some girls who had the brain of a pea between them, had somehow managed to bust the gang out into the open right under Torrey's eyes, in the midst of an investigation.

The raid on Pop's place didn't mean much. But if Torrey had Pop sewed up in some precinct house, the way things were going now, Sanducci couldn't find it out. And if Pop sang, there might be trouble. Sanducci knew he was being watched. He didn't dare go down to headquarters and ask a few questions. First he had to find the gang and ask them.

All in all, it was one hell of a mess, and Allie gave him the creeps. He had to get her out of the way first, and the best way to do that was to give her what she liked best. He lined up another fall guy for her, and drove over to *The Florida*. He went in the back way this time, and waited in the entry, until he was sure he wasn't being tailed. He had to be careful about that, too.

When he knocked on Allie's door, she took long enough answering him. That made him nervous. When she opened the door he slipped right inside and shut it after him.

"Well, what's got into you," she said. She had the camera out on the bed, and there was a box of flashbulbs beside it. She held her fingers up to her lips, to shush him, and she looked real pleased with herself. She was screwing one of the flashbulbs into its socket.

He was beginning to learn what she was like. She could only think of one thing at a time. It was useless to try to get her attention when she was doing something else. He looked at her hopelessly. He had to admit he didn't know how to handle her at all.

Torrey had come for Janey every night now for three nights. They always stayed in there a long time. That was what had given Allie the idea. She didn't know why she was doing it exactly. She just knew she'd feel safer if she had some hold on Janey, now that her other hold was gone. And this one would be a beaut. The thought of it made her grin, and her quick little pointed tongue ran round her lips two or three times.

Sanducci stood in front of her. He cleared his throat.

"Don't," she whispered. She looked up, brushing her hair from her eyes. The bulb was in securely. "They're in there now."

"Who's in there?"

"Janey. Janey's got a boy friend. You'd never guess who." She stood up, smoothed down her skirt automatically, and held the camera gingerly in her hands. She gave him a look of wicked delight. "I hope it goes all right."

"Okay," he said, "what's the gag?"

"There isn't any gag. She's just in there with him, that's all." Her wide eyes were insanely innocent. She giggled, and then put her hand over her mouth. But her eyes did not leave him for an instant.

"It's a dirty trick," he said.

She shrugged her shoulders. "Trick, smick," she said, and bent over the lens aperture, cocking the shutter at the same time. She was in her stocking feet. She began to go over to the connecting door. She had put some kind of oil on the bolt. She eased it noiselessly.

"I haven't time to kid round," he said. "I've got a client lined up for you."

Even that didn't draw her. He went over to her, and took her arm. "Put that thing down and get dressed."

She pouted and wrenched her arm away. "You leave me alone," she said. She knelt down and peered through the keyhole, but apparently she couldn't see much. She listened instead. Both of them heard the creak of the bed, and low murmurs.

"I said stop it," he ordered.

She grinned. "You don't know who it is," she said. "It's that cop friend of yours Torrey. Ain't that funny? How do you suppose she ever latched on to him? And she was always the timid one."

It took a moment to register. It didn't take long. Allie was waiting, crouched by the door, the camera limp in her hand, with one hand on the latch. She was waiting for a promising creak of the bedspring. It came. She shoved back the bolt. Sanducci grabbed the camera from her, kneed her back into the room, so she fell on her back, and flung open the door. He pointed the camera blindly and pulled the shutter release.

Torrey and Janey were not undressed. They were only in each other's arms, and had started up as soon as they heard the noise. Janey looked startled. Torrey looked surprised and angry. He tried to shield her face, but did not have the time. Sanducci was startled too. He had expected something much more. But what he had gotten was quite enough. Allie yelled from the floor.

Sanducci slammed the door and bolted it, just as Torrey hit it with his shoulder. The bolt held.

"Wise guy, what's the big idea?" shouted Allie. She started to get up again. Sanducci kicked her back, and turned the film exposure knob frantically.

"You're wasting my film," wailed Allie. There wasn't any time. Torrey would be after him. Sanducci threw the camera at her.

"Get the film out. Hide it. Have it developed. I'll pay you for it," he shouted.

"What about my date!" wailed Allie.

"I said I'd pay you," shouted Sanducci. Torrey had given up trying to break down the door. That meant he'd be round the other way.

Sanducci was fatter and older than Torrey. He knew what to expect. He wrenched the door open and started down the hall. The door to Janey's room opened, and Torrey shot out. He almost hit Sanducci head on. Sanducci didn't want him to know who he was. He averted his face and made a sprint down the corridor. He wasn't in good condition. It took a lot out of him. He'd never have made it, if it hadn't been for one thing.

Allie's mind worked fast, too. If she could shift the blame on Sanducci, she was just that much better off. She got the roll of film out, holding it tight in her hand, to keep the light from getting at it, and flung the camera after Sanducci.

"There, you rat," she shouted. "Whatya mean busting in here?"

The camera hit Torrey smartly in the back, just as he was grabbing at Sanducci's coat, and knocked him off balance. He didn't bother to look back. He kept on going. But it was enough of an interruption to give Sanducci the advantage. The elevator door was open. Sanducci plunged inside and pressed the down button. The door shut nearly on Torrey's face. Torrey headed for the stairs, but would never catch him.

Allie had a glimpse of Janey's pale white face. She slammed her door and locked it, and leaned against it. Then she licked the red end of the film case, and closed it up.

She was going to have that film developed, but not for Sanducci. She knew what it was worth. At least she had a pretty good idea. She could blackmail him with it.

She smiled foxily, put it in her purse, and listened at the door. She didn't hear anything, but she knew that when Torrey came charging back he'd want explanations. Torrey and Janey didn't interest her now. She had bigger fish to fry. She wanted Sanducci's list of amiable clients. With the photograph to bargain with, she wouldn't have to split with him any more.

Meanwhile she had to get out. Outside her window was the fire escape. Her room was an extra room at the end of the third floor, but on the second floor the fire escape opened into a hall door.

She heard Janey tap on her door, but didn't answer. After a while Janey went away. Allie opened the window and stepped out onto the fire escape.

Ten minutes later she was walking round the corner towards a drugstore with an eight hour developing service. They gave her a receipt, but she did not keep it. If only she knew where the film was, and no one else could find out, she would feel safer. She said she would call to pick it up at noon tomorrow, and left the store, feeling pleased with herself. She felt real clever.

She made two mistakes. In the first place it would be her luck that she had chosen the drugstore from which Pedersen ran his servicycle, which was something she couldn't know.

Second, if she had gone back to the hotel, Torrey might have been able to show her what she was up against. He might even have talked a little sense into that scheming head. But she didn't go back to the hotel that night. First she was afraid to. And second she met a guy who caught her eye.

CHAPTER TWENTY-TWO

WHEN Allie didn't come back by one o'clock, there was nothing for Torrey to do but leave Janey and go home. Besides, he knew no harm would come to her. The harm would come to him, and all he had to do was to wait for it.

He didn't sleep well. When he got up it was gray dawn. His apartment was small, on the second floor of a private house, facing the garden. The garden did not help. He knew what was going to happen to him. He had recognized Sanducci, and he had no illusions about Sanducci. He shaved, had a miserable breakfast, and worried about Janey. He couldn't phone her. She wouldn't be up yet. It was his day off duty. He picked up a sports coat from the back of a chair and hurried out the door, to report to the District Attorney's office. They might have turned up something on Sanducci independently.

The upstairs corridor was cool and shadowy. He did not pay much attention, but clattered down the stairs and out the front door.

The street was a quiet one, lined with tall trees. The houses were on mounds, with lawns dropping steeply down to the sidewalk level. They were old houses, most of them painted cream or white. It was about the most law-abiding, peaceful street in the world, the sort of street collies look at home on.

Outside it was foggier than usual. The moisture clung to his sportscoat and fell shimmering from the trees. Fogs like that were rare. The end of the block was scarcely visible. People loomed suddenly out of the mist and then disappeared. You could hear their footsteps without seeing them. And it was getting thicker all the time.

He couldn't get over the idea that something was wrong. The street had been crowded the night before. He had had to park his car at the end of the block. Now the other cars were gone, but his was still at the end of the block. He couldn't even see it. He walked briskly, and warily. He reached the coupe and bent down to unlock the door.

There was a car parked in front of it. It honked its horn. Torrey paid no attention. The horn went on honking, and held a sustained note. Then it switched its lights on and off rapidly. Torrey stared at it for a while. For some reason he didn't want to go near it. But the horn went on braying away, and something had to be done about that. He couldn't make out whether somebody was inside waiting for him or not. Nor did the car look familiar.

He walked over to it. The far door swung open.

"Get in," said Sanducci.

Torrey hesitated.

"Get in."

"You know what I should do to you," said Torrey, but he got in and closed the door. Sanducci took off immediately.

"From now on in you're not going to do anything to anybody," he said.

Torrey shifted uncomfortably. "I should have beaten you up last night."

Sanducci didn't bother to answer. He twisted the wheel and turned into another street. They drew up in front of a mortuary whose awning appeared out of the mist and swept down to the street. Its green neon sign was on. It made the fog look sick. Sanducci put on the brakes, but he didn't turn off the engine.

He wasn't very pretty when he was on top again. His teeth were yellow and shovel-shaped, like a beaver's. His breath wasn't too good either. He'd been drinking. He still smelled scared.

"How much did you have to pay the girl?" asked Torrey.

Sanducci laughed. "Hell, it was her own idea. I was just dropping by. The point is I got it."

"And what are you going to do with it?"

"That's sorta up to you. I've had you spotted for some time. You don't make any reports to the D.A. any more. And maybe about the others, you made a mistake. Anyhow, when the Grand Jury meets, you quietly get out of town."

"Suppose I don't."

"You will," said Sanducci. "You're a career boy. You don't want to be smeared. It might damage that career of yours. You want to get mixed up with some tart, that's your business. It'd be lovely all over the papers."

Torrey thought it over. But thinking didn't help much.

"You should've wised up in the beginning. You could have had your cut. Now you don't get anything," said Sanducci. "Not a red cent. From now on you do what I tell you."

Torrey stared at the green glow around the mortuary sign. It was hot in the car, and the windshield wipers were going, to keep off the mist. They beat back and forth like a metronome and every once in a while they squeaked. Sanducci was sitting sideways, looking at him.

"It isn't that easy," said Torrey.

"You haven't got anything on me yet. But I've got something on you." Sanducci threw the car into gear, and took off into the fog. He didn't go back to Torrey's car. He kept on driving. Torrey slumped down, thinking to no purpose. "Where are we going?" he asked.

"You were going down to the D.A.'s office, weren't you? Well, I'm driving you."

"What makes you think that?"

"I got friends," said Sanducci. "From now on they're going to like me a lot better." He leaned out of the window and spat. "Unless you'd like to go to your girl friend instead."

"Leave her out of it."

"Boy, she's right smack in the middle of it," said Sanducci. "Brother, you were framed."

Torrey didn't believe it for a minute. If anyone had done the framing, it was Allie and Sanducci. Anything Sanducci had to say in that direction didn't cut any ice at all. And yet he couldn't be quite sure.

The hell of it was that Sanducci knew he couldn't be quite sure and was getting a hell of a kick out of it. Automatically his fists curled up. Sanducci didn't miss that either.

"I haven't got it with me," he said. "Try anything and then see what happens to you."

Torrey sat over in his corner. They drove in silence and then pulled up. Sanducci leaned over him and pushed open the door.

"Okay, golden boy," he said. "I'll be seeing you."

Torrey got out and Sanducci drove off. Torrey went into the building, but while he waited for the elevator he knew he couldn't go through with it. He couldn't fake. He opened the service door and went out through the basement garage to the rear alley. He stopped on the curb, and then walked swiftly through the fog.

It took him twenty minutes to walk across town to *The Florida*. He half expected Sanducci to be following him, but apparently Sanducci wasn't. He went up to the third floor and knocked on Janey's door.

She let him in almost at once. She must have been waiting for him. She was wide-eyed and solemn. As soon as he saw her, he knew she had no part in this frameup. It just wasn't possible. He put his arms around her. It was nice to have someone to hold on to.

After a minute she backed away. She seemed sturdier now. "You're in trouble," she said. "I could feel it."

He sat down in a chair and looked up at her. He just nodded.

"The picture?" she asked.

"Yes."

"You shouldn't have met me."

"That's silly. It's nothing to do with you. Sanducci would have thought of something anyway. You see, he knows we're trying to get him. He has a lot to lose, the way he looks at it."

"What will you do now?"

He spread his hands hopelessly. "What can I do? He's got the damn picture."

She stood against the window, looking at him. "No, he hasn't."

"What?"

"Allie's got it. I think she's gone crazy or something. She came waltzing in here about an hour ago."

"Where is she?" He half stood up, ready to head for the connecting door.

"She went out. She said she'd be back at six. Torrey, she hates me. She's gone off her mind. She'll never let us go. I don't know why she wants me round. But she always does. I guess I'm her audience. Sanducci's got her too. Now she says she's free of him. She's going to hold out on him. With the picture. She's going to make me do things again."

"She can't make you do anything."

"She could ruin you."

"That doesn't matter."

"Of course it matters."

Torrey stood up. "I've got about two thousand in the bank," he said. "We can buy it back. We can get it back somehow, if we have to beat it out of her."

Janey looked at him blankly.

"Okay," he said. "But suppose Sanducci gets to her first? I guess you can imagine what he'll do if she tries any fancy stuff. *We've* got to get to her first."

"Is the picture that important? Couldn't we go away?" she asked.

"Do you know what Sanducci is?" he asked. "Besides, it's my job. I happen to believe in my job. I guess that's unusual for a cop. But I do."

"I'm sorry. Of course you do. I wouldn't like you if you didn't."

He flushed and look at his watch. "We've got five hours to wait," he said. "Can we get food sent up?"

"I can go out and get something."

"Not with Purvis and Pedersen around you can't. We're not taking any chances."

CHAPTER TWENTY-THREE

THEY were a good deal longer than five hours. Allie didn't get back at six.

She was having herself a wonderful time. She thought she was going to make a lot of cash now. She had the money from last night, and what's more the guy was crazy about her. He wanted to see her again.

The fog didn't bother her a bit. It only gave her the creeps. After all, she couldn't know that everyone was after her. And even if she had known it, she'd probably have forgotten about it. She had other fish to fry.

Vera was having *The Florida* watched. Pedersen. Pedersen had a whole flock of side-burned friends who could turn up for a job like that. She was just as glad to have attention turned on Allie, while she set off on errands of her own. The cops were getting too close for comfort. If they got much closer, she might have to frame Sanducci, too.

But having Allie watched didn't mean that they had Allie where they wanted her yet, for Allie walked briskly towards the smart section of town, and there wasn't much the guys could do about her there. If a servicycle circled the block once or twice, she wasn't even aware of it. She didn't notice things like that.

For Allie was feeling satisfied with the world. She had money in her pocket, and there was lots more money where that came from, and from Sanducci's client list, too. She had decided to go out and spend it.

Allie liked crowds, and Allie liked people, and Allie just loved new clothes. It wasn't so much shopping that excited her, as shopping for what she was going to buy next.

It was true, she had been down at the mouth. She had thought she would have to go back to being a waitress or something. She liked men. She had always liked men. But that didn't mean she didn't want to get something out of it, and being a cheap B-girl wasn't exactly up her alley. That was only a beginning. Now the world looked different.

She liked to be by herself. She didn't want to be kept. She was independent. Nobody could own her. But she liked driving in fast convertibles, and going to night clubs, and those people Sanducci had foisted her off on made anyone back in Manteca look like a bunch of hicks. She knew just the kind of apartment she wanted to have. She knew just what she wanted to do.

When she opened a newspaper, back in Manteca, and read about one of those cases that turn up once or twice a year, usually in a big place like San Francisco or Los Angeles, one of those cases where the gambler or tax-evasion case has a "friend" who turns up in court, she always looked at the pictures of the "friend" avidly. Those women had a certain look. They looked like ponies that got rubbed down too often. They dressed beautifully. They never used too much lipstick, they had beautiful furs, and they kept their mouths shut. They had a box at Santa Anita. They knew what made the wheels move round. They had money in the bank. They didn't go outdoors in the daytime, except to shop; they always wore dark glasses; and they always lived with men who were away quite a lot of the time. They polished their own nails.

Then, when they got real old, say thirty-five or so, they still looked young. The men went away. They moved to the Virgin Islands, or something, opened a hotel, and got into Cafe Society.

That was what Allie wanted. She got carried away by the idea. In a week or two she'd open a bank account. Right now she spent three hours buying a gray silk dress and a pair of shoes. She hated to give *The Florida* as her address, but that wouldn't last long. Then she went to the smartest furniture store she could find, the kind that has white plaster rococo tables and Chinese pictures over nine foot sofas, and priced things. She got on fine. She knew just what to do. She liked Joan Crawford in the movies and she could remember every room Joan Crawford had even suffered in.

She had forgotten Janey. She had forgotten Sanducci. She had forgotten the Jickey Club without any effort of will at all. She was supposed to meet the guy she met last night at ten, in the St. Francis hotel, which was big and smart. She was passing by, so she went inside just to see how it felt to walk across the lobby, and she wished her dress was ready. It was to be ready at five-fifteen. She had an almost perfect figure. All they had to do was to do something to the skirt. It was five-ten now, by the lobby clock.

Eventually, of course, she'd have her own apartment up on Nob Hill, on top of the town. She frowned and went to the dress shop.

Half an hour later she was on her way back to the Tenderloin, with the dress box under her arm. She would be late for Janey, but Janey could wait. She didn't have any use for Janey right now. She only wanted to show her the photograph to tease her and get her back into line. Maybe Janey could be her secretary. Sometimes when those "friends" went to court, they had a mother or a companion with them. They always looked like Janey, too, sort of dowdy and whipped, but very nice. Allie giggled.

She still didn't know the town very well. A servicycle whizzed past her, and she didn't even look up. She should have. It was Pedersen. That was a coincidence. Pedersen wasn't looking for her. He was making a delivery. But he saw her. He decided to circle around the block and see what she was up to.

Allie's new shoes had absurdly high heels. She hadn't really learned how to walk in high heels properly yet. Her steps were still too big, and in high heels you have to walk from your pelvis.

She wobbled. Her feet and ankles kept twisting out. But she liked them.

She couldn't quite remember which cross-street the camera shop was on. Someone, she thought, was giving her the eye, a couple of punks behind her or something. She didn't have to bother with that type any more.

Circling the block, Pedersen saw her heading for the drugstore and got the wind up. The drugstore was one of the gang's distribution centers. The manager didn't know anything about it. He thought he just had the usual tough as a delivery boy. But the pimply-faced kid behind the counter with the ducktail haircut was one of Purvis' pals. He was the one who loaded up the prescriptions and handed them over to Pedersen. The dope went out disguised as prescriptions, in the drugstore's own cute little cardboard prescription boxes. It was Vera who had thought that one up.

Allie went into the drugstore.

Pedersen parked the servicycle on the sidewalk, and then went round the alley beside the store, and in the back way. The pimply-faced kid's name was Sammy. He had the load all made up, but right now he was flicking through the film file.

Pedersen slouched in and stamped his feet on the floor. His jacket was thrown over a chair, and his plaid shirt was thick with mist. He put the jacket on, zipped it up, and fastened the studded belt.

"What's she want?" he asked.

"Who, the chippy out front? She just came in for films."

Pedersen scooped up the prescription boxes. "You sure?"

Sammy looked scared. "What else would she want?"

"You know damn well. I think maybe that cop we've got in our pocket is double crossing us, to save his own skin. Anyhow something's gone wrong."

Sammy pulled out the film envelope. His hand was suddenly shaky. "Anyhow, she wants this," he said.

Pedersen stopped him as he was turning to leave. "Hold her a minute. I'll go out front down the alley. Then come through the store with the prescriptions. Crowd her a little. If it's a frame, I can get away with them. Let's see what she does."

Sammy jittered.

"You want to be caught with the stuff on you? Besides, Purvis says maybe we should have a little talk with her. She's up to something."

That was enough for Sammy. He wasn't very bright. He grabbed the film envelope and the prescription boxes and went out front. Allie was looking at the cosmetic counter. "You took long enough," she said.

Sammy kept his eye on the front door. "That'll be one dollar and thirty cents," he said. He saw Pedersen lope out into view, kick the cycle into life, and hold it idling, while he pulled his goggles on.

It made Sammy feel better. Allie gave him a five dollar bill and he made change.

She opened the envelope and pulled out the enlargements. They were eight by ten glossy. A smile spread over her face. Sammy gathered up the prescriptions. "Okay?" he asked.

She looked up at him without seeing him, and then shoved them back into the envelope. "They'll do," she said. She picked up her parcel and turned towards the door, walking briskly. Sammy followed her.

"What do you think you're doing?" she asked. She thought it was some sort of come on.

He motioned with the armful of prescriptions. Allie was in the door. He was eager to get rid of them. He jostled her.

"Hey, look where you're going," she shrilled. Then she saw Pedersen. She stopped on the sidewalk and looked both ways. She looked pale. She decided to make a run for it. She raised the dress box and clouted Sammy with it. He lost his balance. The prescriptions flew through the air. A hypo-needle came out of its box and fell on the pavement.

Allie saw it, and looked up quickly at them. She didn't know what it meant. But Pedersen was jittery. He didn't hesitate.

"Grab her," he said. Sammy was so scared he did as he was told. "Shove her on and kick that stuff down the sewer grid."

Allie opened her mouth.

"Shut up or you'll get it good," snapped Pedersen. "Shove her behind me."

Allie kicked. But fear made Sammy strong. He shoved Allie on the buddy seat behind Pedersen, and Pedersen took off. There weren't any stop signs and it was a one way street. Allie had never been on a cycle before. It got up to fifty awfully fast. The wind stung her eyes.

"Hold still," said Pedersen, "If you don't we'll go over and you'll land on that silly face. That'll really plough you up."

She was still clutching the envelope. "I could scream."

"Try it," he said. "Just go ahead and try it." He went round a corner on two wheels. He stepped up the speed. Allie hung on. There wasn't anything else she could do. Somehow all those pipe dreams of hers faded awfully fast.

"What are you going to do to me?" she asked. She hung on tight.

She was just about ready to have hysterics. The chrome studs on the back of his jacket were cutting into her. He didn't hear her, or if he did he didn't answer.

She hoped for a stoplight. If they hit a stoplight she could make a run for it. But Pedersen knew his city. He wasn't paid to waste gas idling at stoplights, so he knew how to miss them. He didn't hit one.

The air rushed past her, clammy, foggy and suffocating. Any other time it would have excited her. Right now she was scared blue. He took so many side streets, she hadn't any idea where she was going. She'd never seen this part of town.

CHAPTER TWENTY-FOUR

IT WAS SIX and then seven and eight, and Allie didn't come back. Janey was lying on the bed. They hadn't said much to each other. The matter was too serious for that, and they both knew it. It made them shy with each other. The air in the room got close. The light outside the window faded, and Torrey drew the blind. Then they were really alone together. Janey gave him an uncertain smile, and he tried to smile back.

"It'll be all right," he said. He didn't quite know what would be or how. She made no effort to come closer to him. She didn't want to bother him with her own troubles or how she felt about him. After all, all this, as far as she was concerned, was her fault.

There was a lot of street noise. Sometimes, when it was particularly loud, it drowned out the small furtive noises of the hotel. They heard footsteps. Down the corridor a door slammed. They sat forward tensely. But it was always a false alarm. It wasn't Allie.

Torrey began to look worried. His face was tired and gray under his tan, and although Janey searched it for an expression, there was none.

"Don't you have to go on duty?" she asked.

"This is duty. I can phone in later."

She hadn't thought of that, but she supposed it was duty. It made her feel like a criminal. "Oh Torrey," she said.

"What's wrong?"

"Nothing," she said, and bit her lip. His face was so puzzled and he looked so hurt.

"If the picture comes out, will it wreck you?"

He shrugged. "I can do other things." He sounded bitter. "I knew what the risks were. I worked in a grocery store once. I can do it again."

She was suddenly determined. "You won't work in a grocery store," she said. Everything she had ever felt about Allie suddenly formed into a wish to beat her this once. "We'll talk her round somehow."

"Yeah," he said, "if we get the chance." She noticed the "we." They were still together. Inside her something relaxed and felt better.

But they were both very hungry. Torrey looked at his watch. "If somebody doesn't turn up soon, we'll risk it," he said, "and go get some food. You must be starving. We'll wait fifteen minutes."

It was nine minutes later, nine endless minutes, that they heard the elevator coming up. It came up slowly. It might go beyond their floor. But it didn't. The doors rattled, opened noisily, and did not close. Someone must have wedged them. Then there were footsteps down the hall, going quietly but hurriedly. Janey and Torrey looked at each other. The footsteps were heavy ones.

Someone rapped on Allie's door. There was no answer. Then they heard the handle turn.

Torrey put his finger to his lips, and got up. He motioned Janey to follow. They both stood flat against the wall, in the corner, where they couldn't be seen from the connecting door. Torrey put his arm around her. He switched off the lights.

They were just in time. The connecting door opened and someone peered into the room. Torrey could see who it was in the mirror of the bureau, though they were not visible in it, because of the angle. It was Sanducci and he looked angry. The door slammed and he bolted it.

Torrey sighed and relaxed.

They heard furtive movements from next door. A drawer slammed shut. Then the noises grew louder. Sanducci was losing his patience. Janey glanced at Torrey.

"He'll be in here again," he said. "Where can we hide?" He moved towards the door to the hall and turned the knob cautiously.

"There's some sort of service closet by the elevators."

"Good girl," he said, and slipped out through the door. Fortunately the hall was carpeted, though the carpet was thin. She followed him. The door to Allie's room did not open, but they could hear things smashing on the floor. The utility closet was not locked. With a glance behind him, Torrey slipped inside. She followed him. It was a tight squeeze, and the closet smelled of disinfectant. It was so small she had to stand with her feet in a slop pail. He held her tight, and she was glad of that. She hated the dark. She had a terror of being shut up in it.

Fifteen minutes passed. She could just see the red sweep hand glowing on Torrey's watch. Then they heard footsteps again. The elevator door clanged shut. Sanducci passed so close to them that they could hear him breathing heavily. He was muttering to himself. The elevator went down.

They both let out a long breath, and Torrey reached for the door. It had a small twist knob on the inside. His hands must have been sweating. It took him two tries to get the door open, and they tumbled out into the hall and went right down to Allie's room, and her own. Sanducci hadn't even bothered to close the doors.

Janey glanced into her own room, and then gasped with dismay.

"Yeah," said Torrey. "He must be desperate."

They stepped inside. The door had been wrecked. All her clothes were pulled out of the closet and flung on the floor. The bedding was thrown in all directions and the mattress was upended. The drawers of the dresser were hanging half out of their slots. She looked at Torrey quickly, and then went on to Allie's room.

Here the chaos was even worse. Sanducci hadn't merely been looking for something. He'd been blowing off steam. Clothing was hanging everywhere, even stockings from the chandelier. He had ripped up the dresses, with a hasty fury that wasn't pretty to see. He had even torn up the rug, and gutted the pillows. The pictures he had smashed, to get at their backing faster. There was broken glass all over the floor. He had kicked the drawers to pieces.

Janey sat down weakly on the bed.

"Wherever it was, it wasn't here," said Torrey. "Could she have hidden it in your room?"

Janey looked at him vaguely. This was the first she had ever seen of real violence.

"What?" she asked.

"The picture."

"She didn't have it. It wasn't going to be ready until this afternoon. The eight hour service broke down or something. She just described it to me."

"Then he didn't get it. She has it."

"Wherever she is," said Janey.

His face fell again. He looked dashed.

Janey was thinking. She sat with her face in her hands, and stared at the room. "We've got to find her first," she said, "don't we?"

"That's the idea. But she could be anywhere. With anybody. Where do we begin?" He looked round the room helplessly.

Janey looked round it too. Then she got up and began to poke around forlornly.

"What is it?" he asked.

"Allie kept a diary. She showed it to me sometimes. She never showed it to anybody else. Sanducci wouldn't know about it."

"How will that help?"

"She kept a list of every man she went out with and what happened and what she thought of him." She flushed. "She was businesslike about it. She might be hiding. If she is, where would she go? Do you see?"

He saw. They both began to hunt. It took them quite a while. At last they found it under a pile of movie magazines Sanducci had thrown into the closet. It was a thin leatherette square fastened with a flap lock. Torrey sat down on the bed and started to rip it open. Janey made an instinctive movement.

"Suppose he finds her first," he said. "If we get her, I'll buy her a new one." He stuck his forefinger under the flap and yanked. The leatherette was cheap. It came away at once.

They sat side by side and went through the book. It didn't make very nice reading. Allie didn't trust herself with anyone, but she did trust herself with the diary. She was certainly proud about the false pregnancy, and taking Janey in, and all that. She didn't think much of Janey either. Reading, Janey flushed. But there was no time to think of that. They began to skip through, in search of names.

They found them.

"Come on," said Torrey. He couldn't leave her behind. Sanducci might be back. Janey didn't know anything, but if Sanducci thought she did, she wouldn't have a very good time. "Grab your coat."

They got her coat off the floor in her room, and went to the elevator. In the lobby Torrey had to make a phone call. Janey watched his face through the glass of the booth. It changed expression rapidly. He smiled at her hurriedly, hung up, and dialed another number.

He talked quite a while. Then he came out of the booth.

"Things are happening," he said.

She gave him a worried look.

"Sanducci hasn't reported in for duty. And something funny happened round here. They couldn't get Sanducci so they were trying to get me. Where did Allie leave that film?"

"I don't know. Somewhere near I think."

"There's a drugstore round the corner. About six o'clock something strange happened there. The clerk came out with a girl. It sounds like Allie. The delivery boy was outside. There was some sort of fracas. They shoved the girl on the servicycle and the driver took off." He shook his head. "So did the clerk, only in a different direction. They haven't found him. The prescriptions got thrown in the street. Only they weren't all prescriptions."

"What do you mean?"

"Dope," he said. "Heroin. They're holding the owner, but they don't think he knows anything about it." He paused. "The delivery boy was Pedersen, if you remember who he is. One of the characters at the Jickey Club."

"Oh." She looked round the empty lobby. "What do we do now?"

He held out the book with a sigh. "I guess we start with Sparkman. He's mixed up with that gang some way, or was once. He might know where they'd take her."

Janey blinked. "Heroin?"

"Yeah. It's a drug. We've been after that, too. We've had our eyes on them. But we never caught them. Somebody protects them."

"Sanducci?"

He made a face. "Your guess is as good as mine."

"But what will they do to her?" she asked.

He shrugged. It wasn't a very reassuring shrug. She drew closer to him.

CHAPTER TWENTY-FIVE

PEDERSEN hadn't lost his head. Pedersen never did. He knew exactly where he was taking her.

The fog was thicker. They seemed to be heading into it. Allie had lapsed into a tight, sullen silence. It was her usual defense when she was scared. She hung on to him tightly. They began to go downhill, into still heavier swirling mist. The air smelled different. The buildings here were old and of brick. They were long, four story warehouses with an abandoned look.

This was an abandoned part of the city, though she didn't know that. It was called Aquatic Park. Parts of it had become smart, but it still had an empty look, even when it was crowded with Sunday people.

The city had made a half-hearted attempt to turn it into a playground. Like most city projects, once it was done it was left to rot. There was a large white building shaped like a pair of upended binoculars. In the basement was a lavatory and a storeroom. Upstairs there was a Marine Museum. A tier of concrete outdoor stairs did for sunbathing. Behind the building some old Italians were always playing bowls. A semi-circular jetty with a narrow path on top of it served to enclose a small bay within San Francisco Bay itself. The water was yellow, black, and gray. Layers of slime and old newspaper and mud floated at different levels in the water. The water was tired. It only fingered the edge of the very dirty artificial beach. Rocks close to a sea wall were coated with slime. Small children played here. On a sloping lawn everybody in the district who was at a loose end came to sunbathe, if there was any sun, and just to sit, if there wasn't. It was a lonely place. There was a Seascout base at one end. Next to it there was a hotdog stand. Moored between them was the riverboat, listing badly. It looked as though it had been washed up there, and in a sense it had. Some promoters had bought it to turn into a restaurant casino. So far they hadn't been able to do that yet. It dated from the 1880's. It was derelict. It was also private property. Nobody was allowed aboard.

Pedersen came down the hill, and coasted to turn a corner. He wasn't taking any chances. He bumped over the curb, at about thirty-five, and rode down the almost deserted walk. Then he cut the engine. Allie was too shaken up to make a run for it, and besides she didn't know where to run to. Pedersen didn't give her the time for a second thought. He jumped off and grabbed her from behind, twisting her wrist. But first he honked his horn real loud, three times in a row.

"Walk," he said. He looked rapidly around him, but because of the thick swirling fog, the pathway was almost deserted. There was only a tall, thin man walking away at the far limit of visibility. He turned, stared for a moment, attracted by the cycle engine, and then moved on.

Pedersen gave Allie a shove and turned her wrist. She winced and blinked her eyes. She had gotten something in them during the ride, which hadn't worked out. It hurt and made her eyes water. She couldn't see very well. She made no sound. She didn't dare.

In front of her loomed the huge curved wall of the lee side of the ferryboat. It was four stories high, with the superstructure on top of that. It was so tilted, that the wall rose up outward from her. The white paint was peeling and blistering. So was the wood. The windows on what would have been the street level were painted over. It was utterly lifeless.

A narrow, rotten plank lead from the stone retaining wall to a side sliding panel in the wall of the boat. He forced her across it. They were about eight feet above the water level, and it was low tide. She looked down. Below here were jagged, slime-covered rocks and ripped beer cans. The plank wobbled. She edged her way forward, just ahead of him. He did not let go of her. Once she stopped.

"I can't stand heights," she whimpered.

He just grinned and gave her wrist another twist. She moved on, wobbling on her high heels. The plank was only about ten or twelve feet long. She reached the lip or flange of the boat, pressing up against the door. There they stood, while the fog dashed and swirled around them. Pedersen banged and pounded on the door with his free hand.

He was clearly nervous. He didn't want to be seen. He stamped up and down impatiently, but he kept between her and the gangway. His pale eyes were almost transparent.

At last they heard something drop somewhere inside, and shuffling footsteps. A chain dropped and the door slid open. Pedersen shoved her in so hard she fell full length on the floor, right over a tangle of rusty old elbow-bends from dismantled sinks. He jumped in after her and pulled the door closed, locked it, and pocketed the key.

The man who had opened the door didn't like that. He made a quick gesture and then thought better of it. He was about sixty, immensely tall and thin, so thin that his bones stuck out at all the joints. He was wearing faded dungarees with bell bottoms, a faded blue shirt too small for him, and a greasy yachting cap. He hadn't shaved for days, and the stubble was dirty yellow-white. His eyes were so small that they seemed to be shrinking all the time, and his flabby, dead-white skin was covered with faded tattoos that were rose-red and sickly green. Some of the tattoos had run. Some of them had faded. Some of them had blobbed. They were the color of the veins and arteries too close to his skin. There were dragons and hearts and anchors and dancing girls in picture hats, dating from 1900. And smack on top of all of them, on his upper arm, was a brand new scrambling panther with a red tongue, about six inches long, not counting the tail. He walked with a shuffling stoop and his voice was a whine.

He looked down at Allie without interest, his eyes badly out of focus, and he kept sniffing and twitching all the time.

"Who's she?" he asked.

Allie had torn her stocking. Her knee stuck through it. And one of the heels had come off her pumps. She sat up and glowered at them.

Pedersen just laughed and prodded her with his boot until she got up. "That's better," he said.

"You shouldn't oughta bring your tricks here, you know that," whined the man.

"She isn't a trick. She just needs cooling off for a while, cap," said Pedersen. "Where can we put her?"

"I don't like all this. It ain't safe," whined Cap.

Pedersen shrugged. "How's Pop?"

"He's still out cold. I locked him in, like you said." Cap's whine was watery. He didn't have much fight in him.

"Come on, I ain't got all day," said Pedersen. "The cycle's outside. We don't want anybody nosing round."

Cap shuffled to one side. "Give me my key."

"Nothing doing. You can stay in with the menagerie for a while."

Cap looked weepy, but he turned and shuffled off. Pedersen kept Allie ahead of him again. He had his knife out now. He felt better.

The only light came from a sliding door open to the bay on the far side. The floor sloped steeply. They were on the cargo level. Slim columns held up the ceiling. They were cast iron with corn husk capitals. The floor was littered with plaster, chicken wire, a bashed in life boat, and old plumbing fixtures, the guts of a couple of beds, and lengths of pipe. There were two big openings in the floor. One was filled with dark green oily water. The other showed machinery far down, rusted and broken up. They went up some narrow stairs. The main stairs were outside, and they didn't want to be seen. They had to work their way through the interior.

Allie knew she couldn't do anything right away, but she looked around her. She had to escape. It wouldn't do any harm to take a look round for something that might help. She didn't think much of Cap. She could take care of him easily. If Pedersen went away for a while, she might have a chance.

But she didn't see anything that might help. She was too bewildered, and she had never been on a ship before.

They went up a narrow staircase and came out into the ruins of an immense mahogany salon two stories high, and almost the length of the boat. Lifesize mermaids from the pillars of a dismantled bar stretched up their arms from the floor. What light came in from the smashed skylights glittered on their tight dry breasts. Above their heads the inner walls had been ripped from the staterooms on the decks above. Shutters, bedsteads, and plaster hung out in space. The light was gray and dim. At the far end of the hall rose a wide curved staircase with missing banisters.

They forced her to them. They went up steeply and crazily. One riser was missing. She held on to the banister, but the banister gave under her hand, and stood springing back and forth in space. She hurried on to the top. The top was some sort of lounge. In a corner was a card table with several metal chairs around it. From the windows she could see the shore. But the glass was thick and solid. It was three stories up, and the drop from the deck would be straight down to the rocks. She turned to face them.

Pedersen chuckled. "You don't look so good now," he said. "You looked real good when you went to the drugstore."

She said nothing. She looked at Cap. But Cap wasn't going to be any help. He was twitching more than ever.

Pedersen left him there and pointed to an entrance way. "Down there," he said.

Allie held back. She didn't have any idea what he had in mind. She must have showed it.

"Don't worry," he said. "You aren't going to get hurt—yet." He prodded her to the entrance.

It opened onto a long corridor, which ran down the length of the boat. Louvered doors lined it. Those on the right were shut. Those on the left were open. These opened onto the ruined cabins over the main salon. Pedersen followed her glance and smiled.

"Cap's cooperative. Sometimes we have gang-bangs here," he told her. "With real girls, it's fun. Nobody can hear anything from outside."

Allie had glanced at a bed with torn sheets, half hanging in space. She walked on, reluctantly. But he was right behind her. They reached the end of the corridor. He leaned around her and shoved open a door.

"In," he said.

She didn't like the look of it. She went in. He closed the door and locked it. But it was a thin door. It wouldn't be hard for her to break it down as soon as he was gone.

Behind her someone snored.

She whirled round, and gave a gasp.

"That's just Pop," he said. "He's in cold storage, too. He won't bother you."

The room was dim. It had only one soot covered port hole high up in a corner, and too small to crawl through. It was finished in solid mahogany like the rest. It was surrounded with benches. In the center was a stout column. On one of the benches a figure lay crumpled up with its shoes off. It was Pop, all right. Pop wasn't a man whose appearance you would forget.

"He's dead drunk," said Pedersen. "That way he behaves." He reached inside his jacket and began to finger his belt. He was wearing the chain. The links clanked through his hands. She had every reason to remember that chain. She started behind the column.

She lost her footing, stumbled, and half fell over Pop. He hardly stirred. She screamed.

"Go ahead," he said. "No one will hear you." He grabbed her and slapped her twice, hard. She sobbed. "I'm not going to hurt you now. I haven't the time." He pushed her against the column, and holding her with his flexed knee, swung the chain around her waist. He pulled it tight. "Hold your breath in," he said. He kneed her more firmly, and she drew her breasts up. He pulled hard, as though he were cinching a horse. He was sweating from the effort, and he was right on top of her, holding her arms tight at her sides. The chain had a slip fastener. He clicked it over the fifth link from the end and padlocked it. Then he backed off. She tried to scratch him. But when she leaned forward to scratch at him, the chain cut her so much she gasped.

"Yeah," he said. He went to the door. "You'll stay put. And just in case you'd any ideas about Cap, he's a mainliner. Just so he gets his dose, he doesn't care about a thing. It's real convenient."

He gave a mock wriggle at her, went out, and locked the door. She heard his heavy footsteps down the corridor. He was whistling off key. Then there was silence.

She started to squirm, but squirming didn't help.

There was no sound but the slow uneasy creak of the boat, and the occasional cry of a gull. The column, like everything else on the boat, was on a tilt. By leaning against it, she could ache less, but the chain cut into her flesh. She heard the cycle start up.

There was some movement behind her. She half twisted round. It was Pop. He was up on his feet, with a silly smile on his face. He staggered towards her. He began to giggle. He giggled and giggled and giggled. He was in one of his own movies. There was no mistaking what he was up to.

She tried to get free. She couldn't. Then, just as he was about to reach her, he keeled over drunk again, and lay face up at her feet. One of his hands grasped her ankle. It held on as only a drunk can hold on. Then, abruptly, it relaxed.

She thought maybe he was dead. She screamed. But Pedersen was right. No one could hear her. There was only a dull echo in the room.

CHAPTER TWENTY-SIX

FOLLOWING SPARKMAN was a hunch. Besides they had to start somewhere. He wasn't too hard to find. He was listed in the phone book. Naturally they went to that address. They didn't know anything about his hideaway at the motel. That was something Sanducci had kept to himself.

There was a file on Sparkman down at headquarters. It was confidential, but Torrey had seen it. He had never been arrested. But he had been stopped by the police once or twice, in highly questionable circumstances. Whenever the police did that, they took the name and address, and added it to the confidential file. Then, if they ever did really nail somebody on a charge, they had a certain amount of previous suspicions to bring forward. People like Sparkman always get in a jam eventually. Then when the defense attorney brings forward temporary insanity, the District Attorney can always ask why the police were so suspicious back in 1936. A lot of poor devils get sent up that way. Or then again, if somebody murdered him or beat him up, they'd know why.

Sparkman's house turned out to be a typical San Francisco style home with the garage underneath. It was out towards the Sunset District, near the ocean, and was well kept up.

As they pulled up before it and Janey got out, she glanced up and saw some movement of the flounced curtains at the front of the house. A moon face suddenly disappeared. She had scarcely seen it long enough to recognize it. She stared up at the window. The left hand curtain swayed a little bit and was still. That was all.

She said nothing about this to Torrey. She did not quite know why not. He took her arm and they went into the entry and up the stairs.

As they were about to ring the bell, the door opened and two children came charging around them, and vanished down the turn of the stairs. They were a boy and a girl, about five and seven. They were pretty children. Janey looked after them and then glanced up.

A woman was standing at the door. She was about forty-three or four. She had a pleasant determined face, but her breasts were flat and she was wearing sensible shoes. Her hands were thin and nervous. Somewhere behind that set expression of her face there was the ghost of a smile. Those eyes could light up if they wanted to.

She seemed to take their appearance for granted.

"I thought I'd better send the children out to play. They're very young," she said. "You'd better come in."

She was trembling slightly. She turned and led them into a pleasant living room. It was furnished with taste. It was comfortable, but it was not much lived in. She sat down on the sofa, folded her hands in her lap, and faced them. Now that the children were out of the house she seemed to feel relieved. Instinctively Janey felt sorry for her.

There was a short silence.

"You have come about my husband," said the woman at last.

"We're trying to find him. We thought he might be here."

Something happened to Mrs. Sparkman's eyes. But she did not move.

"What has he done now."

"Nothing. He may know about someone."

"Whatever he does, it's only himself he hurts," said Mrs. Sparkman. She turned to Janey. "I suppose you want money. Well, I don't have any money." Her eyes wandered round the room. "I know where he goes for his amusements. If you were there, then you're no better than he is." Her mouth became tighter. "You needn't think this hasn't happened before. And I have had to deal with it before."

"Mrs. Sparkman, you don't understand," began Torrey.

Mrs. Sparkman looked weary. "I've lived with it for ten years. There is very little I don't understand by now." She sighed. "He can't help it. It does no harm. But why should the children suffer?" She leaned forward intently. "I won't have the children suffer. And I can't pay you. Now get out."

Torrey looked uncomfortable. The room was too tense. Janey didn't know what to say.

"We don't want your husband. But we have to find him," said Torrey. "He may know where someone is. Someone who's in danger. We have to find her."

"You're from the police."

"Yes."

The doorbell rang. Mrs. Sparkman went to answer it. They could see her and hear her. It was one of the children back. He had forgotten his ball. Mrs. Sparkman told him to go play and come back for it later.

"I want it," said the boy. He darted betweeen her legs.

"Johnny, come back here," snapped Mrs. Sparkman. The boy half turned to face her. He looked frightened. Then his jaw set and he ran towards the back of the house. Mrs. Sparkman followed him.

From the back of the house came a clumsy crash, as though someone had fallen downstairs. Torrey got up and ran towards the back of the house. Janey followed him.

Mrs. Sparkman was in the kitchen. The room was a shambles. Spools of film and stacks of magazines and photographs stood in front of the stove. She had been burning them. The lid was off the stove. As now one and another reel of film caught, it gave a muffled pop and the green flame leaped up through the stove lid hole. Mrs. Sparkman had her back to the basement door. She leaned over and threw the key into the stove.

Torrey pushed her aside and flung himself at the door. They heard noises in the basement. Someone was sliding up the garage doors. Torrey tugged at the door and then rammed his shoulder against it. The panel splintered a little.

Johnny ran into the room. "Hey Mom," he said, and then looked round the kitchen. Another reel of film popped and the flame danced.

"Get out," shouted Mrs. Sparkman. "Go to your room." Suddenly she couldn't keep herself in any longer. She screamed and began to shake. Janey moved instinctively towards her.

Johnny did not move.

"Go to your room," shouted Mrs. Sparkman again. Johnny looked frightened. Janey took his hand. It was sweating. She knelt down in front of him. "There, there," she said. "Be a good boy. Do as your mother says. Go on."

Uncertainly Johnny turned and went down the corridor.

Torrey split the panel, and reached through to unlock the door. But it was too late. Below them they heard the car roar out of the garage.

Mrs. Sparkman leaned against the pile of magazines and photographs. It gave and ran slithering across the floor. It didn't leave much to the imagination, even at a casual glance. She stooped down and flung more of them into the fire, tearing them savagely.

"Why does he have to be this way," she shrieked. "Why does he have to be this way?"

Torrey made a motion to Janey and went out into the hall. In a moment Janey heard him asking the operator for headquarters.

She put her arms around Mrs. Sparkman, who was very thin under her dress. But there wasn't much she could do.

"Nothing's going to happen to your husband," she said. "Truly."

Mrs. Sparkman tried to control herself. She looked up.

Why does he have to be that way?" she demanded. "He knows I'll stick by him. Why can't he tell me? He's so good to the children. He's even good to me. I don't understand. He came in this morning, and he looked hunted. Like an animal. After all, they're just pictures. What harm can pictures do?"

Torrey came back from the hall. "They'll phone back," he said. "I told them not to stop him. Just to let me know where he was going." He glanced at Mrs. Sparkman. "Can you make her lie down? Maybe there's a sedative in the bathroom or something."

Mrs. Sparkman looked at him. "You're not going to arrest him?"

"Of course not. Not for this, anyway."

"That other policeman had threatened to. I know that."

"What other policeman?"

"I don't know. I only saw him once. Dark and flabby looking. I don't know what his name was. He drove my husband back here once or twice. He scared me."

Torrey looked at Janey. He knew what policeman. They both did. Janey took Mrs. Sparkman into her bathroom. There was no sign of Johnny. When she came back Torrey was standing over the fire, feeding in the pictures. He glanced up at her.

"How is she?"

"She's resting."

Torrey held her arm reassuringly. "This is quite a workout for you," he said.

"It's all right. What are you doing?"

"Burning the stuff." He looked sheepish. "Why should she have any more trouble?" He went on feeding the film into the fire. Neither of them spoke. They must have stood there for almost fifteen minutes.

"She loves him," said Janey.

"Yes, I guess she does." Torrey gave her a rapid glance. "Don't look at that stuff."

Janey blushed. "It's hard not to." She toed the pile of photographs. "Allie's bad, isn't she?"

"I'm afraid so."

"She was my friend, though. She really was."

"Some friend," said Torrey shortly.

Janey didn't say anything.

The phone rang. Torrey put the lid back on the stove and went to answer it. He came back to the kitchen in a hurry.

"They've spotted his car down at Aquatic Park. He was trying to get into the boat down there. I told them to hold it until I got there." He turned back towards the front door.

"I'm coming, too," said Janey.

He looked at her for a moment. "It might be dangerous. "Why don't you stay with Mrs. Sparkman?"

"That's why I'm coming."

He frowned, hesitated, and then smiled. "Okay," he said, and held out his hand. "Let's go."

CHAPTER TWENTY-SEVEN

THE BOAT was never still. Allie was doped with fear and pain, but even so she could hear it. To her other fears was added the fear of being swept out to sea. For she didn't know anything about ships and she had never seen the ocean. She listened carefully. But except for the screaming of the gulls, she couldn't hear any sound from the outside world at all.

Her waist was numb. She felt as though her legs would drop off. It was dim in the cabin now. She had no idea how much time had passed. She was dying of thirst and she was bitterly hungry. Once she heard shuffling footsteps at the door. She yelled. But it was only Cap. He chuckled. He went on chuckling for quite some time. Then he moved away, with the same slow shuffle. On the floor Pop did not stir. In the gathering darkness he seemed to loom larger. She kicked to free her foot. She wanted to stamp on his hand, out of sheer fury, but she was afraid to wake him up.

Pedersen had certainly tied her up good. From time to time she wriggled to get free, but she knew she couldn't. Having her hands loose was just a joke. She couldn't snake out of the chain. She bruised her skin and pinched it, trying to do so. She couldn't break the links or the clasp. Finally, just to rest her aching body, she clasped her hands behind the pillar, for support, until her arms went to sleep too.

Suddenly, one of the portholes darkened. There was a face at it. It went away.

Then she heard noises. She did not know whether they were coming to set her free or to get her, or even if they knew that she was there at all. She was too hysterical to reason that out. She knew now that for once in her life she had gotten into company too fast for her. But she was also determined that somehow she'd get even with them. If she was whittled down to her last thought, that was the last thought she would have. She squirmed to face towards the door.

She heard whispering somewhere outside. It was quick, hot, angry whispering. The voices moved away. Then they moved closer again. She heard the key rattle in the lock. The door opened. But whoever it was had no lights. She couldn't tell who it was.

But she recognized that assured walk and the click of those heels.

"Pedersen," said Vera, "didn't anyone ever tell you not to over do it?"

Vera came closer. Allie had her eyes closed. Vera slapped her. Allie's eyes flipped open and she stared back. Vera drew away.

"Well, well," she said. "The question is now, what do we do with her?"

The cabin was littered with cane-backed chairs. Vera dragged one up and sat in it. So did Purvis and Pedersen. There was a silence. It was filled only by Pedersen drumming the horseshoe plates of his boots against the floor.

Allie could only half make them out. Purvis was chewing gum. He was also sweating. In the semi-darkness he looked like a diseased rabbit. And one thing showed in his narrow little eyes. He was scared. Therefore he hated her. His eyes were vacant. He always looked at you as though you weren't there. At first she'd thought maybe he took dope. But that wasn't it. It wasn't even the way he sang. It was just that as far as he was concerned there wasn't anybody in the world anywhere. There was just Purvis.

He'd do anything to keep Purvis on top. She knew that now. It gave her the shakes.

Pedersen was better, but not much. She just had to look at Pedersen to know that Pedersen wouldn't stop at anything. Purvis might be scared, but Pedersen would just go through with it, whatever it was. He was going to go through with it now.

That left Vera.

"Get rid of Pop," said Vera.

"He's out cold. How?"

"Take him out and stack him in the hall. Drag him by his heels."

Pedersen did as he was told. Pop didn't even wake up. Then he came back and sat down.

"Okay," said Vera. "Talk."

"What about?"

"Anything you think we'd like to hear," snapped Vera. She scraped her chair closer.

Looking at her, Allie realized that Vera knew she didn't know anything. That she was just playing with her, for some reason of her own, and enjoying it very much. Allie licked her lips.

"What do you want me to say?" she quavered.

"Just the truth, honey," said Purvis. "Just the simple truth. Such as why you just happened to be going by when Pedersen here was making a shipment."

Vera smiled. Not at the others, for they couldn't see her, but a private little smile that only Allie saw. And Allie didn't like it.

She shook her head helplessly.

Purvis jumped up and slapped her so hard she thought her neck would break.

"How much did you tell Sanducci?" he shouted. "How much?" He hit her again. "When's he going to rat on us?"

Again Vera gave that odd, pitying smile. It was as though she were watching the dangerous games of a bunch of children. And that was silly. She was only twenty herself. Yet somehow she wasn't like Allie. She wasn't even a woman. She wasn't any age.

"Yes," she said. "How much?" She bit her nails. "Tell the boys how much."

There was some kind of racket somewhere down in the hold of the ship. It echoed beneath them.

"What the hell," said Purvis, and half got up. He was pouting. Pedersen headed for the door.

"Hey," said Vera. "Let her loose."

Pedersen stopped.

"Go on. We don't want her found this way."

"She'll make a run for it."

"By this time she can't even walk. Come on."

Pedersen did as he was told. Vera was right. Allie could scarcely stand up. She stood there, rubbing her waist and leaning against the column. The others turned towards the door, ready to run, but it was too late for them to run.

Steps pattered down the hall, and Sparkman burst into the room. He almost fell on top of them. It was a different Sparkman. He wasn't dapper any more, and his skin hung in folds, as though most of the fat were sweated out of him.

"What the hell do you mean by coming here?" demanded Vera.

"I had to come somewhere." His voice sank to a whine. "I was scared. The police came to the house."

"What's that to us?"

"They're after me." He looked round him uncertainly. "I came to warn you."

"You ran to save your own neck," said Vera. She didn't seem interested in him. "And probably you brought the whole damn Vice Squad down on ours."

"No I didn't." His eyes flickered past her and he saw Allie. If he recognized her he didn't say anything.

"Come on," said Vera. "We're clearing out. It's too hot here."

"That's Pop out in the hall," said Sparkman. "What've you done to Pop?"

"He's drunk, that's all."

Purvis looked up. "Suppose they search the ship," he said.

"Suppose they do?"

"There's stuff here. You know. It came in last week. Cap told me."

"Shut up," snapped Vera. She hesitated. "Where?"

"Down in the hold."

Vera sighed. "Throw it overboard. Come on. We haven't much time." She turned towards Allie. "We certainly owe you a lot, sister," she said. "Right now we can't pay you back, but we'll think of something."

"Bring her?" asked Pedersen.

"Yeah. Bring her."

He shoved Allie ahead of him. They went down the corridor. It was hard for her to move, but she knew she had to make a break for it. But the corridor was narrow and they all walked in a clump. Purvis was out in front. They had forgotten Pop. Purvis was in a hurry, and they just naturally followed him. The ship was creaking again. They were all nervous now. They reached the stairs and started down them. They went faster. That gave Allie more room. But she didn't get a chance to get away. At the foot of the stairs to the hold Purvis stepped into a side room. They could hear him ripping away the paneling. Then he came back with a small packet. He threw it over the side.

"All that money," he said.

"It wasn't your money," snapped Vera. She was on edge now. Sparkman was shaking. He drew away from them.

"Well, what's with you?" demanded Pedersen.

"I'm staying here. It's safe here."

"It isn't safe anywhere," said Pedersen. "The trouble with you is, you know too much. Who introduced us to Cap?"

"That isn't my fault," said Sparkman. He was so scared he didn't know what he was saying.

"Nobody's blaming you. But nobody's leaving you behind to blab either."

Sparkman looked from one to the other of them. Then, with a sob, he whirled and clattered down the stairs. They were all jumpy. It was enough to set them off. They were after him. Allie didn't have the strength to get away herself. Besides, Vera was right there beside her.

Sparkman reached the cargo hold. It was vast and shadowy. He got ahead of them. There were a lot of places to hide down there. But Sparkman wasn't exactly a silent man. They could hear him weeping.

"Fan out," said Vera. "Quick."

It was Pedersen who spotted him. Pedersen had cat eyes. He gave a shout and the others came up. Sparkman was near one of the water-filled holds. He gasped when he was spotted, bent down, and picked up a length of pipe.

"Hell, he's crazy," said Pedersen. "He's just scared blue."

"Get him," breathed Vera.

"Oh sure, I'll get him." Pedersen picked up a piece of pipe, crouched down, and began to stalk Sparkman, getting closer, and making quick feints with his piece of pipe. Sparkman backed away, until he was against the rim of the hold.

"Come to baby," said Pedersen. "That's nice." His voice was wheedling and contemptuous. He was getting ready to strike.

Sparkman shook his head. Tears were running down his cheeks.

"You can't hurt me," he screamed. "I've got a wife and a couple of kids. I don't know a thing."

"You blab," said Pedersen. Suddenly he threw the lead pipe at Sparkman. Sparkman was too slow to fend it off. It hit him square on the chin, but so hard it knocked him backwards. He disappeared and then there was a splash. He had fallen into the green slimy water in the hold. The sides were smooth. The climbing stanchions had rotted away. Pedersen went to the edge and looked down. Sparkman went under, came up, screamed, and went under.

"Leave him," said Vera.

"He'll drown down there." Pedersen sounded angry.

"Let him," snapped Vera. She shoved Allie towards the door. "We haven't the time to bother.

Allie swallowed hard. Now she knew too much, too.

"You don't want him to drown," said Pedersen. "You got witnesses."

"It was an accident," said Vera. "Come on." She gave Allie a shove. "You, too."

CHAPTER TWENTY-EIGHT

Sanducci's world was caving in.

Personally he'd always thought he was a pretty good guy. In fact he even thought he was a pretty good cop, as well. Of course some people might not agree with his definition, either way. But so far some people were something he never had to worry about.

Now he did have to worry about them. They were closing in on him. They had him on the run. He didn't even dare go home to get a clean shirt. Instead he had to hole up in some cheap motel.

Sanducci blamed it on the gang.

He had to blame it on something, for he didn't think the D.A. had anything against him personally. Every once in a while a town thinks it would like to clean up vice. But usually the Vice Squad takes care of that, and it's all in the family. This time it wasn't in the family. But he hated to see something he'd spent ten years building up, collapse overnight. He hung on as long as he could. In his own way he went round asking questions.

Sanducci was a machineman. The machine had lodged him in the Vice Squad and that was okay with him. The machine had been out of power for about ten years now, but Sanducci had his toehold and he kept it. He learned the ropes. Nobody touched him. Maybe he relaxed too much. Most cops do.

Now he was holed up in a motel out in Polk Gulch, under another name, and it was driving him crazy. He spent the night on the telephone. By midnight he had all the information he needed, and it made him hate Torrey's guts. He also had a police radio in his car. Every once in a while he went downstairs and sat in it, to see what he could find out.

He was sitting in it when he heard the call go out to stand by for special duty down at Aquatic Park. He heard something about not moving in on the show boat. That was enough for him. He knew his game was up. If the gang was caught, the gang would talk.

He didn't quite know what to do about it. That is he didn't know how to stave it off much longer. He knew he would need help. He checked out of the motel, just so no questions would be asked later when he didn't turn up, got into his car, and drove downtown, biting his nails at every stoplight. It was beginning to rain. Not much, but enough to show the night would get worse instead of better.

He left the radio turned on, but low, so nobody would hear the police calls. He expected another bulletin. But there wasn't another bulletin. Maybe they thought he was listening in. Everyone knew he had the radio. If an alert came out for him, they wouldn't broadcast it.

He'd always meant to get some phony papers from Pop. But somehow he'd never gotten around to it. It was too late for that now. Pop might be anywhere, and blabbing his mouth off about more than was good for any of them.

The light changed and he drove on. He had driven automatically to the Tenderloin, but he knew nobody down there would be apt to help him out. From time to time he'd squeezed them too hard. But that wasn't why they wouldn't help out. It was because now they wouldn't be afraid of him any more.

He had Torrey to thank for that. He cursed. The car skidded in the rain. It was thicker now.

He'd spent so much of his life making contacts, that it had never even occurred to him before that contacts weren't quite the same as friends. Friends were people who paid you off. There wasn't even a tart somewhere whom he could trust. Not even

Vera. But then he never had trusted Vera. That made him smile. He knew where he was heading now. He swung the car around. Some sixth sense made him feel he should hurry.

For one thing, if they raided the show boat, that left one place for Vera to go. He wanted to get there first. For even though nobody knew about the place, now that her gang was getting busted up, the place wouldn't be unknown much longer. Vera would certainly try to hole up there, and if she was as frantic as he was, he didn't want her poking around.

Vera couldn't have been more than fifteen the first time she was hauled in to the Station. No one had led her astray into vice. It was all her own idea. She'd had a body and she'd known what it was worth. She was a wise one. She'd taken the knowledge one step further. She'd realized that other girls had bodies, too, and that she could get a percentage. He picked her out of the line-up right away. He'd smoothed things over. Then he'd dug down to see what he could get on her. He got plenty. She already had a gang of high school girls. She had even started off on her Chinese contacts. The Chinese, she'd figured, would be less apt to squawk or tip over the applecart by getting moral. She had been right.

He didn't get anything on her. So he made a deal with her instead. He wanted a house, but he didn't want to own it openly. He got her to rent it for him. It was handy. She could use it, he said, as long as she kept her girls out of it, and as long as he could have it twenty-four hours on Thursdays and when he needed it. That was just a blind. Actually the house was his bank. Most cops who made a little on the side got caught through their bank accounts. The house was his bank account. It didn't pay interest, but at least it was safe.

He'd had the carpenters in before he even told her about the place. His money was safe, and there was a hundred thousand out there. As long as the investigation kept undercover a while longer there would be enough to get him out and let him lie low.

There were other things out there, too. He had to destroy them. And he had to get there before she could. Because sometimes, he knew, she had Purvis out there, and the gang, for a gang-bang. It would be where they'd all go. Now that they were on the run. And if the gang went, that was where the cops would go, too.

The rain was heavier, and his windshield wiper wasn't working so well. He put on speed. The house was way out by the sea cliffs, south of town, near the county border. When he'd bought it it had been isolated. Now it was surrounded with a mushroom housing development of little huts colored every color of the rainbow.

It was a good forty-five minute drive. He stepped on it, and cursed every red light along the way.

He was doing fifty-five when he drove over the broken glass. It wasn't small glass. It was big chunks. Some truck had slipped a couple of carbonated water flasks. Both rear tires went at once. He skidded to a stop somehow, with one front wheel up on the curb, hopped out, took a look, and cursed. The rain was fierce now. It blew through the fog in great gusts. Way up the road he saw the pink and green shimmer of a filling station. There was nothing to do but hike it, and tell them to hurry it up. He set off; desperate, and for once wishing he hadn't been so cheap about getting a new set of tires.

CHAPTER TWENTY-NINE

Actually the patrol car wasn't waiting outside. Torrey had asked them to keep an eye on the boat. That meant they could circle the block or go somewhere else and come back. The car was moving away slowly, uphill, with its searchlight on, just as the gang came out of the show boat.

All they had to do was walk quickly along the shadowy walk, and bundle Allie into the car. She found herself flung in back, with Vera on one side and Purvis on the other. The driver was someone she didn't know, but he was some other member of the gang. He had the black and yellow wasp jacket they all wore.

Pedersen leaned through the window and said he'd follow on the servicycle. If he got ahead, he'd meet them at the house.

Vera didn't like that. "We can't go there."

"Why not? Where else would we go?" He eyed her narrowly. "You wouldn't be planning to rat out would you?"

"The same goes for you," snapped Vera.

Purvis' face was taut and white. He was humming to himself. He always did that when things were going bad. And right now they couldn't go much worse.

Pedersen spat. "Yeah," he said.

Vera started to speak, and then thought better of it. She leaned back in the seat.

"That's better," said Pedersen.

"What do you mean by that?" she asked sharply.

He shrugged and moved away. Purvis watched him go, and Purvis didn't like it. Purvis didn't like to be without his bodyguard, and he didn't trust anybody very much. "He know something I don't?" he asked.

"It wouldn't be hard," snapped Vera. She drew into herself. But she was certainly nervous. Her arms were crossed, and a muscle in one of them kept twitching.

Allie stared straight ahead of her. For all she could see of where they were going, she might just as well have been blind-folded. Vera drew back into shadow. For some reason this trip seemed to be upsetting Vera very much.

It was a long ride, and the car had no heater. It was cold. They could hear the servicycle behind them. Sometimes its head-light raked across them. The driver, whoever he was, didn't have anything to say either. But he drove rapidly and well, skidding expertly round corners when he had to. Soon the neon signs were left behind. They began to go through street after street of identi-cal houses, all built tight against each other. The smell of the air changed. They were getting near the sea.

The houses thinned out. Ghostly trees stood against the rain. The paving here was worse. Then they shot into another housing development, with its shopping center shut up tight. On the other side of the housing development a low hillside covered with scrub swept off into absolutely nothing. To their left was an old farmhouse, guarded by two tall cypress trees. To their right were two stucco houses, left over from a building boom that had failed. Grass grew in the old street, and the earth had forced the curbing loose. The car stopped. Vera and Purvis bundled her out.

They had parked inside a hedge. In front of them an old wood Gothic house with bay windows loomed up through the rain. The air was full of iodine and salt. A dirt path, full of mud now, led down the cliff. The porch of the house was broken in. There was a light inside somewhere, it was hard to tell where. A couple of cycles were parked near the porch. One had a tarp over it. The other didn't. Through the rain came the dim echo of a radio playing away to itself.

Vera made a dash for the house. Purvis followed her, just as Pedersen drew up. He wasn't careful about it. If Allie had any stockings left, the mud from his wheels took care of them. She swerved aside.

"Who told your friends to come here tonight, of all nights?" demanded Vera. She'd taken the car keys from the driver. They swung angrily in her hand.

Pedersen shrugged. "Search me."

"What are you up to anyhow?"

Pedersen cut his engine. "You're just jumpy, that's all," he said blandly. But he didn't take his eyes off her for a minute. He swung off the machine. "On the other hand, what are you up to?"

Vera didn't answer. She marched into the house and left the others to follow.

The front rooms were unfurnished. The radio came from somewhere out in back. Vera went down the hall and in at the far door. She was real mad.

The room was a porch with full length windows looking out at absolutely nothing, it was so dark. It must be on posts over the cliff. It had a shabby rug and newspapers all over the floor. It was a shambles.

The driver of the car was right behind her. As soon as he saw who was in the room he brightened up. They were pals. They had black and yellow wasps painted on the backs of their jackets. Now he knew where he stood.

"Hi," he said. He sounded relaxed. "What's going on?"

Vera glared at them, but they didn't pay any attention. They were used to her. She was just someone you had to put up with if you knew Purvis and Pedersen.

"Gang-bang. Only we haven't got girls," said one of them.

"We got a girl," said the driver.

"That's just Vera."

"Get up," shouted Vera. "Who told you to come out here?"

"We didn't need no invite, Vera," said the first of the three guys sprawled on the sofa. He was holding a beer can, and there were empties on the floor and an open cardboard case by the radio. They were Pedersen's motorcycle crowd, half drunk and ready for anything.

But one of them wasn't that drunk, the first one who had spoken, Bob. He was a big rangy guy with long tapering fingers, a two days' beard, and glittering transparent eyes that made him look like a hound dog with rabies. He seemed relaxed, but his whole body was tensed to spring. He looked at Pedersen questioningly.

"Hey, who's the babe?" asked the second one, as Allie came in. "She's a little beat up, but she's okay."

Allie leaned against the wall and stared at them. They made quite a picture, but it wasn't a picture that made her feel any better. When they got wild, they'd be dangerous.

"I said, who told you to come out here," snapped Vera.

"Friend Pedersen, if you care. We've been here before. What's eating you?"

Vera swung on Pedersen. "Why?"

Pedersen grinned at her. "Ah can it," he said. "The boys have to drink somewhere."

Vera looked ready to choke. "Don't crowd me. Don't ever try that," she said. But there wasn't anything she could do about it and she knew it. The room was against her. Purvis reached over for a beer. "Why don't we play my records?" he said.

"Put that down," snapped Vera. "We gotta talk."

"Honey, we've had a talk," said Purvis. "And where did it get us? We're safe here. Nobody's going to find us here."

Vera stamped out into the hall. Purvis followed her. That left Allie and Pedersen. "You, too, honey," he said. His face was watchful. He waved to the boys. "Stick around," he said. "I might need you."

Out in the hall he blinked amiably. "Let's dump her," he said. He shoved Allie into a room and slammed the door on her. She heard it lock. Automatically she looked round for a way out.

There wasn't any.

It was a small room with flowered wallpaper that had been peeling off for twenty years. There were two tiny round windows high up on one wall. Probably it had once been a dressing room between two bedrooms. There were two other doors, both locked. One of them had a full length mirror. The only other thing in the room was a cast-iron double bed with a mattress on it. One corner of the mattress was eaten away. The stuffing was the color of boiled brains, and had the same rolypoly texture.

Allie sat down on it. There wasn't anything else for her to do. She'd seen Sparkman go backwards into the tank. She knew what to expect.

After a while she heard a murmur of voices. It came from next door. The house was cheaply built, and the walls thin. But here the walls must be thicker. She couldn't hear very well. And she knew she had to hear. She went over to the door on that side, the one with the mirror, and peered through the keyhole.

It was another room like this one, but better furnished. In fact it was a real room. Vera, Purvis and Pedersen were in there, having a council of war.

She couldn't hear much. But she could hear enough, and what she heard stopped her dead in her tracks. She moaned.

For, of course, they had to get rid of her. It wasn't just Sanducci, and how he might be using her to break them up. She'd seen what amounted to murder. Now she really had something to talk about.

It made the three of them solemn. Murder was something they hadn't counted on. Sparkman had been different. That was just something that had happened. Nobody was to blame for that. But outright murder was something else again. It made them angry with each other. They wanted to wriggle out of it if they could, or anyhow put it off as long as they could.

The trouble was they might not have much time.

Vera blamed Pedersen.

Pedersen wasn't upset a bit. "Honey, I seem to be getting on your nerves," he said. "Now why would that be?"

"You're stupid," snapped Vera. She was twitching with impatience. She glanced at her watch.

"You in a hurry about something honey?"

She ignored him. "I might've known you'd louse things up some way. Just plain stupid."

"Maybe I'm not as stupid as you think."

"What's that supposed to mean?"

Pedersen shrugged. "I got eyes, too. Two of them," he said.

Vera didn't want to go on with that one. "Which one of us?" she said.

"Why don't you do something for a change? I should think you'd like that. After all, she tried to get Purvis-boy away from you."

"You leave me out of it," shrilled Purvis.

"You scared?" asked Pedersen mildly.

"It isn't my sort of thing, that's all."

Pedersen eyed him for a while. "No," he said after a while. "I guess maybe not. You don't like the rough spots much, do you?"

Purvis didn't say anything. But he looked ready to cry. He glanced round the room jerkily.

"There isn't any way out," said Pedersen. "This one we go through with. So do you."

There was some kind of commotion outside Allie's door, the one Pedersen had locked. She turned round and faced it. The key did not turn, though. In the next room Pedersen got up. She heard the chair scrape, and his heavy boots in the hall.

It must have been Bob, the one with the transparent eyes. He began to pound on the door.

"Hey, what'ya think you're doing?" asked Pedersen.

"You got a girl in there, haven't you? I need a girl. I don't think she'd complain."

There was a silence. Then she heard Pedersen laugh. "Well, it's an idea at that," he said. "But maybe we should wait a while." She heard their footsteps sound heavily down the hall. The radio went up. Apparently Purvis and Vera had followed them, too. From time to time she could hear laughter from the front of the house. That was all.

Time went by. She couldn't believe it. Yet she knew it was true. They were going to kill her, and she didn't have a chance. She tried both the doors. She couldn't budge them, either way. She clawed at them. All she did was break her nail. It was very dark. Something gave. She pressed again, over and over again, desperately, until her shoulder felt like mincemeat. She needed a hairpin or something. She took one out and fiddled in the lock. It was something she had never done before, and she didn't know how to do it. She lost all count of time. At last the lock clicked. But so did the latch on the door to the corridor. She dropped the pin, terrified anyone would see it, and turned to the door.

She knew who it was, all right. He stank of sweat and she knew that smell. It was Pedersen. The others were right behind him. They filled the door. For a minute they stared at each other.

"I guess you know what you've got coming," said Petersen. His voice was thick. "Me and the boys thought maybe you might as well have a little fun first."

They were drunker than beer could make them. Vera must have spiked their drinks. Vera would be good at that. Pedersen edged closer. The other two and Bob shoved after him. They let out a whoop. They were real worked up.

Pedersen grinned and shoved them back. He shoved so hard they went down on the corridor floor in a tumble of boots. "One at a time," he said. "Whose idea was this, anyhow?"

"Mine," said Bob. But he didn't seem to hold a grudge. He was amused.

Pedersen was less amused. "She can take it," he said. "She just loves it. And I need it more than you do."

Suddenly Vera was standing outside. "Hey, you leave her be," she shouted. But she didn't look displeased. She looked as though everything was turning out just the way she wanted it. Her face got a cunning look.

Pedersen slammed the door in her face, locked it, and turned to Allie. "After me, honey, the boys'll be a real relief," he said.

Allie backed away and screamed.

"Go right ahead," he said. "I like it that way."

He began to stalk her down the narrow length of the room. He wobbled. But he wasn't nearly so drunk as he looked.

Outside Vera heard the scream and smiled. Then she went back to the living room. She had to tape Purvis down next. She had a lot to do and not much time to do it in.

The boys were in there, but they weren't paying much attention. They were making jokes about Pedersen and Allie.

Purvis was sitting on the sofa, alone, with his eyes closed, and a slow, lazy, dreamy look on his face. His face was pale and his lips trembled. He was happy.

He turned off the radio and put on the phonograph. Every time Purvis got a little ahead of the game, he went down and cut a record of himself singing something, preferably a song he'd written himself, and a small combo that played the way he told it to. Nobody ever paid much attention to him, but Purvis liked to sing. That's how he'd gotten in with Vera in the first place. If you wanted to sing you needed money. You needed lots of jazzy clothes and a barber who really knew what to do with hair, and all the rest of it. You needed publicity and publicity cost money. If you were a singer you needed a Cadillac. And then somehow one thing had led to another, but he had the clothes now, and his records sounded swell.

Vera looked at him pityingly. She was badly rattled by now. What she really wanted to do was lift up the record and smash it. But she had to keep her head a while longer. The last of Purvis was something she could hardly wait to see. But that could be managed too.

She sat down beside him.

"That's new," she said.

"It's long playing. It lasts half an hour." He didn't open his eyes.

When he got like this, there wasn't much she could do with him.

"Which one of you's going to do it?" she asked.

The gang looked up curiously. But Purvis didn't even answer. She could have shook him. Then she realized that if the record lasted half an hour, he'd stay glued to it for half an hour, and that took care of him. She looked round the room. The others were too dumb to notice anything. She got up and went down the corridor to the furnished room, and locked the door.

Through the wall she could hear Pedersen making a lot of noise, so he wouldn't bother her for a while either. Quietly she pushed back a chair and began to turn back the rug.

She'd found out about Sanducci's cache a long time ago, when she needed one of her own, and she didn't intend to leave without it.

CHAPTER THIRTY

THE FOG had begun to lift, but the rain was thicker. It romped down the hills towards the bay. Those hills were steep. It made driving dangerous.

Torrey skidded down the hill towards Aquatic Park, just as the patrol car cruised out from a side street, without lights. He drew up and honked and the patrol car drew up alongside. He jumped out and went over to talk to them. Janey's window was down. She could hear them plainly.

"What's been going on down there?" asked Torrey.

"The guy went in. He hasn't come out. His car's still down there. The brown coupe. You want help?"

Torrey shook his head. He looked down the hill towards the show boat looming up whitely at them. It certainly didn't look inviting. "Stick around though. If I don't come back in twenty minutes, you'd better come in."

He came back to the car and got in. The two patrolmen looked at Janey curiously. She shrank back. Torrey didn't even notice the look. The patrol car slid down to the foot of the hill like a clumsy beetle. They followed.

"Stay here," said Torrey, and slid out of the car. She opened the door on her side and followed him. He tried to make her stay back. "There's no telling what we'll find," he said. And yet he seemed glad to have her.

They walked along the deserted, rainswept path to where the board crossed over to the entrance door. He helped her across it. Fortunately he had brought a flashlight with him. That helped some. He tried the door and it was not fastened. He pushed it aside.

She peered over his shoulder into the pitch dark restless hold. "Would Allie be here?" she asked.

"Who knows?" He looked at her for a moment. "I'd rather you turned back. You can wait in the car."

"No."

"Good girl," he said, put his arm around her, and kissed her. They went inside.

Even with the flashlight, it wasn't easy to find their way. They could hear the restless slap of water. There was something not quite right with the sound. It was hard to tell what. The rain beat in through the cargo door on the bay side. The junk strewn on the floor made walking no easier. And of course they had no way of knowing whether anybody was watching them or not. They might be covered.

They edged their way along. They could see the stair at the far end, as a lighter patch to head towards. Between them and it, loomed the rim of the hold over the old boiler room. They bumped into it, and Torrey pointed his flash downward. The ray shot down the oily water, catching the machinery. Then it caught something else.

"What is it?" Janey asked.

"Nothing," he said. "Better not look." But his voice was hard, and she did look. It was the body of Sparkman, floating on the oil slick. As she stared, it gracefully swayed over and she could see the face. Even in death she could see the panic.

She thought of Mrs. Sparkman, at the stove, burning up all those photographs. She gasped.

"Yeah," said Torrey. He didn't have to say anything else. She stuck close to him now. They went up the stairs cautiously, and down the length of the dismantled bar and restaurant above. The boat was restless in the rain. The wall-less cabins above them were a good place to set up an ambush. Torrey tried to hug the wall, but mostly there wasn't any wall to hug. They kept stumbling over debris. Ahead of them rose the main stairs, the balustrade hanging in space.

If anybody was aboard, he was keeping awfully quiet about it. But Sparkman's body meant something. Sparkman's body meant someone was desperate. Torrey half expected it to be Sanducci. He had to tie in with this somewhere.

He put out a hand, switched off the torch, and held Janey. He listened eagerly, but there was no sound, except the eerie night sounds of the boat. The staircase was bright enough from its skylight. They began to edge their way up. They reached the top.

Someone was sitting silhouetted against the window. They stopped where they were. They drew back against the wall. But the figure did not move. With an impatient sound, Torrey went forward. Still the figure did not move, and it looked dead. It just had that dead feeling. He flicked on the flash.

It was Cap. He was out cold. There was an empty fifth on the table, and that told the story. Torrey held up his head, and slapped him. But the eyes were vacant. He hadn't been able to get a shot. So he'd gotten soused instead. In his condition, liquor would send him out like a light. He didn't even groan.

"Well, that's that," said Torrey. "He won't be able to talk for hours."

Janey was scared stiff. "Listen," she said.

They listened. It was a faint sound. But it was a human sound. It came from down the corridor. Torrey took off down it, and Janey followed him. Pop wasn't moving round much. They almost fell over him. Torrey turned on his flash, and made an exclamation. "So that's where he hid out," he said. He squatted down. "Recognize him?"

Janey nodded.

"He might talk, if we can bring him to," said Torrey. He looked at Pop narrowly. "Certainly Sparkman can't tell us anything."

"We've got to get those pictures," said Janey. "We've just got to."

"I'm afraid it's bigger than that now," said Torrey. Suddenly he leaned over and cuffed Pop with the flashlight, right across the nose. Pop's eyes flew open. "Faking," said Torrey bitterly. "Not that he isn't drunk as the other one. But then he's used to it. Where's the girl?" he asked.

Pop merely looked at him, and drew into himself.

"They went away."

"Where?"

Pop looked cunning. It made him seem shy. "How would I know?"

"You know. Or if you don't you've got a pretty good idea."

"They'd kill me."

"Yeah, I guess they would," snapped Torrey. "Come on, get up."

"What for?" Pop stared at him. "Hey, who are you anyway?"

"Cop," said Torrey.

Pop didn't say anything.

"I said get up," ordered Torrey. He stood up, and toed Pop's body. He was really angry. Maybe he over did it. Anyhow Pop crawled up the wall, until he was more or less erect.

"What are you going to do to me?" he asked.

"That depends," said Torrey. He spun him around and headed him down the corridor. "Get moving." Pop moved, and Torrey kept right behind him. They passed Cap in his chair. That startled Pop.

"Dead?" he asked.

"He might just as well be."

"It's Pedersen," said Pop. He might be up and moving, but he really was drunk. He was also cunning. Half way down the stairs, he kicked Torrey and made a run for it. Torrey cursed and half fell. But Pop wasn't having an easy time of it either; He tripped and fell too. Torrey jumped him from about the fifth stair. The fight didn't last long. There really wasn't much fight in Pop, only fear. But it didn't put Torrey in any better mood. They went on, down the narrow stairway to the entrance level.

Torrey shoved him over to the rim of the cargo hold and flashed the flashlight down on Sparkman's body.

Pop was scared. "What're you going to do to me?"

"Look."

Pop looked. Sparkman's little moustache had curled up at each end. It looked as though a little black bat had settled down to suck all the blood out of his body. The water lapped gently against what was left of him. It was enough for Pop.

"Now talk," said Torrey.

"I can't. I don't know anything. They'd kill me."

"Maybe Sparkman felt the same way. Where are they?"

Pop just shook his head.

Torrey slapped him with the flashlight. "Where are they?"

"I'd have to show you," said Pop. "I really don't know what it's called. I've only been there once."

Torrey looked at him and made up his mind. "Okay," he said. "Get moving."

"I want protection."

"You'll get it. In the pokey."

Pop didn't like that. "It's that guy Pedersen. I said that," said Pop. "I didn't know anything. I was hiding here, see. I was drunk."

"And so?"

Pop told them as much as he could remember of what had happened. Allie tied up, and Pedersen, and all. It wasn't even nice to listen to. By the time they reached the plank, he had gotten it all out.

Once on shore, they plodded through the rain. The patrol car turned on its searchlight and picked them up. They walked down the beam to the car. They were soaking wet.

Torrey talked through the door. "There's a body in there. And a guy called Cap. You'd better pick them up and have someone watch the place. And let me use your radio."

The cop at the wheel got out and Torrey slid in. He put in a general riot call, with Pop to tell them roughly where to meet. The instructions were to creep up silently, and then go on to the house. He finished and got out of the car.

"Okay boys," he said, and shoved Pop into his own car. Janey didn't get in. Behind her the patrol car was already edging farther downhill. It stopped and the two cops went into the showboat. The morgue ambulance would be along later. She shivered.

"Now what?" demanded Torrey.

"You don't want me along. The whole thing will come out. You can't explain me. I don't want to get you into trouble."

"Let me handle that," said Torrey. Something like compassion flickered across his face. But it was much more than compassion. "Get in, or you'll get pneumonia."

She got in. He drove off, staring straight ahead of him, ignoring Pop. "You may as well get used to it," he said. "I'm standing by you. I'm not going to lose you now."

"Suppose Allie talks?"

"She may not get the chance," he said tautly, and drove on through the rain.

Pop said nothing.

CHAPTER THIRTY-ONE

I T TOOK SANDUCCI a long time to get the flat fixed, and he didn't dare use the police radio while the garage man was working on the wheel. When he did turn the radio on, he didn't hear anything much. He drove real fast. It did seem to him that there were more patrol cars around than usual, and they seemed to get thicker. It wasn't until he had almost reached the hideaway that he picked up the message about the rendezvous. It was a guarded message, but he knew what it meant. It meant he didn't have much time.

He didn't dare drive right in. He left the car on the far side of the house. But the hedge was solid. That meant he had to walk round the front. He was too fat to make much of a walker, and he was wearing tight shoes. He floundered in the puddles and the mud.

He was almost to the porch, before he spotted the car and the cycles. That stopped him in his tracks, and he cursed. He'd always suspected that Vera used the place as a gang hideout, but this was no time to find out he was right. He didn't trust Vera. For all he knew she might have rounded up reenforcements just for him. He didn't think she knew what he had hidden out here, but she might.

He ran for cover, and then moved his way round the side of the house. In this downpour he didn't have to worry about making too much noise, but it was so dark he had trouble picking his way. The radio became audible, as he approached the back. He peered into the window, and saw Pedersen's motorcycle pals laid out on the chairs and sofa. He didn't see Vera, but as he watched, Purvis and Pedersen came in the door. He ducked and went round the side of the house.

There were three windows here, two of them only about four feet off the ground, one of them small and high up. Sanducci wasn't scared of many people, but he was scared of Pedersen, and he didn't have a gun. He'd have to get in quietly. There was a light in the window of the room he wanted. He could peer in. It was empty. But the window didn't open, for the good reason that he had once nailed it up, and the louver shutters on the inside were fixed in place too. He'd done that to prevent anybody breaking in.

The other two windows were dark, but the second was high up in the wall, and very small. The third one was also dark. It was too high for him to raise, even if it had been unlocked. He had to risk it. He fumbled round for a rock and smashed it. Then, tensely, he waited. But there was no movement inside the house. Gingerly he got his hand inside and eased up the sash, until he could push it up from outside. Then he got his heavy, flabby body half over the sill, and tumbled into the room, easing himself on his hands.

He needed a weapon, and he found one. It was an old bourbon bottle. He grasped it firmly by the neck, and it made him feel better. All that exertion had winded him. He got to his feet and headed for the door, just as he heard someone scrabbling at it. He braced himself and stood waiting. He'd cut his hands on the glass, badly, and the blood oozed down over his fingers. It made it hard to grasp the bottle firmly. But he hadn't time to wipe it off now.

Then the door opened and the light caught him. He was half turned round. He raised the bottle and made a dive for the door.

It was Allie. The boys hadn't exactly been gentle with her, and not only had there been four of them, but Pedersen was original. He wasn't exactly brutal, but he had ideas. They'd had their fun. Now they were in the living room, getting drunk enough to do her in. A few more drinks and they might find that fun too. She didn't. She had maybe ten minutes to save her life. She pulled down her skirt, put on her shoes, grabbed her bag, and clawed open the door. She was totally unprepared for someone on the other side of it.

Sanducci hit her head on. She didn't say a word. She thought it was one of the boys. The wind was knocked out of her. She went down in a heap.

Sanducci bent over her, saw who it was, and clubbed her. He didn't dare try the door to the hall. Instead he took a running lunge at the connecting door, and hit it with his shoulder. Sanducci weighed at least two hundred and fifty pounds. The door splintered away from the lock, and he wrenched it open.

Vera had the rug up. She was crouching down over a hole in the floor, lifting out a black tin box. She didn't even have a chance to look up. He rushed her. She fell sprawling over backwards on the floor. The lid of the box flew off, and money slithered all over the boards and the rug.

He drew back, panting, and hastily began to scoop the money back into the box. Neither of them said anything. Vera watched him. Her bosom went up and down.

She laughed. That was exactly what she would do. It was a low, throaty laugh, and she sounded as though she meant it. Maybe she did. Under her makeup, her face had that slightly dead, slightly Oriental calm, North Italians often have. Nothing could shake her up. Or at any rate nothing had so far.

"We could split," she said.

Sanducci grunted and went on gathering in his cash. "How the hell did you find it was here?"

"I'm not stupid. You had to hide it somewhere. I said we could split, or didn't you hear me?"

"Why should we?"

"Keep your voice down," snapped Vera. "Pedersen has his whole gang of toughs out there. All I have to do is scream. Just one scream. They'd make mincemeat out of you."

"You too."

"What?" she asked.

"You were running out on them, weren't you? Pedersen hates your guts. He does whatever Purvis tells him to."

"Purvis does what I tell him to. What anybody tells him to. He's spineless. Pedersen doesn't exactly love you, either."

"You cheap two-timing bitch." Sanducci had almost finished. He paused to glare at her.

"Do I scream or don't I?"

Sanducci hesitated. She smiled. Then they both heard footsteps down the hall, heavy footsteps. The boys were coming for Allie. Vera and Sanducci didn't say a word. Both of them had forgotten about the splintered door.

The drunken boots stopped in the corridor, outside Allie's room. Whoever it was was whispering and laughing, but it was sort of scared laughter. A key rattled in the lock. They heard Purvis whining. Purvis didn't sound happy at all.

"You're elected," said Pedersen. "You may as well grow up sometime, and it's time you did our own dirty work. Then we know you're really one of the boys." They heard Purvis stumble. He must have been shoved into the room.

The door slammed on him and locked. But the footsteps didn't go away.

Suddenly Vera and Sanducci both remembered the splintered door. They froze.

They heard Purvis mumbling to himself. "Hey, where are you?" he called. There was no answer from Allie. Vera looked at Sanducci. Sanducci was afraid to move, but his hand reached for one of the closed boxes in the hole. He knew when it was time to move along.

Purvis stood in the middle of the room and gave a real holler. He was acting for the kids outside, of course. Then he loomed up in the splintered door. He had a length of lead pipe in his hand,

and his knuckles were white around it. He was edgy. He was all ready to do something really wild.

You couldn't blame him. He'd never killed anybody before.

It took him a minute to take in the scene. You could see what he was thinking moving across his face. Then he raised the pipe, whirled it round his head, and charged them. "Pedersen," he shouted. "Pedersen."

Vera ducked, but she wasn't quite fast enough. He hit her a glancing blow on the arm.

"Pedersen!"

Heavy boots tramped down the hall. And then somewhere outside they all heard the siren. All except Purvis. He was really after her.

Allie had come to. She lay where Sanducci had shoved her. She heard the siren, too. She reached for her purse, and pulled herself along the floor of the third room, and over to the window. She hauled herself up.

Pedersen didn't come. The boots raced out the front door. Outside the servicycle choked and then started into life. Sanducci picked up the unopened cash box and made a run for the spare room. He was through the window so fast he scarcely noticed Allie.

Purvis hesitated. "Pedersen," he yelled again. But there wasn't any answer. Just the roar of the cycles. He flung the pipe at Vera, whimpered, and ran for the door. He really made it fast. Vera didn't follow. The pipe got her right across the forehead.

He tore out into the yard. Bob was having trouble with his cycle. He couldn't kick it over. Purvis didn't waste any time. He socked him in the neck, pushed him off, and jumped on.

Down the hill the siren got louder. He got the thing going and took off. Bob lay face down in the mud. Purvis didn't even notice. He wasn't much good at cycles, and the ground was slippery underfoot. He had enough on his hands. He was so scared he began to sing.

CHAPTER THIRTY-TWO

THE SIREN was a mistake. Some of these local police just couldn't keep their hands off the siren. It made them feel important, maybe.

Everything was going fine. The rendezvous went off without a hitch. They found four patrol cars and two motorcycles waiting near the supermarket on the edge of the housing development. Torrey couldn't get out and leave Pop alone with Janey. He blinked his lights and finally one of the lieutenants came ambling over to him. One of the cycles circled in, too. Torrey showed his credentials, and told them the layout, as Pop had told it to him. If they thought the whole thing was pretty unusual, they didn't say so. But they took Janey in, all right. She didn't say a word. She did try to smile.

Then they moved off again. With that many police around, Pop didn't seem as scared as he had been. Besides, he was singing for favors now. He was almost talkative.

They swung out towards the bluff with its three houses. The rain hadn't let up a bit. They had to go carefully. Pop pointed out the house. Torrey braked to flash his tail-lights, as a signal to the others behind. He started up the hill. Everything was going smoothly. And then that damn fool let loose with his siren.

Torrey stepped on the gas. The car skidded in the mud, shimmeying sideways across the road. He couldn't hold it above thirty. So they went ahead at thirty. They heard the servicycle start up, too. Torrey cursed and turned his headlights on high, as he swung between the yew hedge and into the driveway. The servicycle was headed right for him. The light of its headlight, and of that of the other two cycles, was blinding. All he could do was step on the brakes and pray. The cycles swerved, circled, and headed up the side of the house, over a rough dirt path that led towards the edge of the cliff. Torrey swung on up to the house.

As he did so, his headlights caught a figure scrambling out of a side window. It was unmistakably Allie. Torrey slammed on the brakes and made a dash for the house. Janey didn't follow. She knew she had to get those pictures. She ran for the side of the house and Allie. Allie still had a purse with her. And if Janey knew Allie, the pictures would be in the purse.

Torrey shouted after her, but she didn't even listen. She kicked off her shoes and ran through the mud and the bushes, whose thorns tore at her stockings.

"Allie," she shouted. "Allie. Stop. Wait."

Behind her someone else dropped from the house. She felt something hit her. The uproar of the cycles was deafening, and they were just ahead of her. She swerved aside, and went right on. Allie's figure was silhouetted for an instant against the side of the cliff. Then she disappeared. Janey followed. The path led to the left and was very narrow. She could see the cycles moving down it. A searchlight swept her. The highway patrol cyclists had figured out what had happened. They were bumping after her, feeling their way. Pedersen and the gang knew these trails. They didn't.

There was a steep yellow slash in the cliff, and down this Allie had plunged. There was no sign of her. The sand below was almost black. It was foggy. Janey could hear the surf, but not see it. But she had to get the contents of that bag before the police did. Torrey shouldn't have to face that. Without stopping to think she plunged down the gash.

The path was too narrow for Pedersen. He had had to circle back. He always had been a daredevil and hill-climbs were a specialty of his. He'd had his lights off. Now he gunned out of the bushes and headed right down the cliff face behind her.

The patrolmen didn't dare follow. They pointed their search-light beams straight down. Janey ran to the left. They fired. But Pedersen was too fast for them. He slipped and slithered to the bottom, still right side up, and headed down the beach, out of the beams' way. Janey shouted for Allie and got no answer. The other cycles hit the beach farther down. They, too, had switched off their lights. The highway patrol boys started down the trail.

CHAPTER THIRTY-THREE

ALLIE slipped in the yellow adobe mud, and slid down to the beach on her bottom. For a second she just lay there, too surprised and too hurt to move. She was staggering to her feet when Pedersen roared past her. He was going too fast to stop, but he was only a foot away from her. He saw her all right. What light there was glinted in his eyes. She knew he'd be back. The patrol lights still streamed down the cliff. Someone had been shouting for her. Someone was following her. Allie sobbed, stumbled to her feet, and ran.

Out of the searchlights, she was blind as a bat, and she certainly wasn't used to walking on sand. She kicked her shoes off, what was left of them, and ran. She didn't know where she was going. She only knew she didn't dare stay where Pedersen had last seen her.

The rain was thinning out, but the fog was worse. She heard the ocean pounding to her left. And the Pacific isn't a gentle ocean along that coast. It's cold, dangerous, and wild. Even a wave on the shore, if it's strong enough, can suck you under.

The beach was almost a cove. At the far end it was stopped by cliffs. It was perhaps half a mile long. At the south end one could get out up an arroyo. The middle of the beach was humpbacked. The winds and the sea had piled up a sand dune that ran from one end to the other. Between the dune and the surf at high tide was a strip between two and five feet wide. At low tide it was much wider, but right now the tide was not only full, but angry as well. The waves pounded invisibly.

A man loomed up in front of Allie. He was too heavy set to be Pedersen. She realized she didn't only have Pedersen to look out for. She ducked, and in ducking, stumbled over a driftwood log, and fell on her chin.

At the sound the man whirled and ran the other way. She knew who it was now. It must be Sanducci. He was carrying something. Down the face of the cliff crept the patrol cycles. They didn't turn off their lights. They needed them. From time to time the beams lit up the beach and the swirling fog. They lit up Sanducci now, and his figure cast a glaring fat shadow. The two cycles on the beach must have realized which end of the beach they were at. She could hear them returning. That would be more of Pedersen's boys. They headed for the surf. They were invisible. Allie gasped, got up, and staggered to the top of the dune. One of the cycles was churning through the surf. She could hear it splutter, and the foam danced in the air. It was coming nearer. She couldn't figure out where Pedersen was. Behind her she could hear someone running and calling out to her.

It only made her run the faster. She thought it was Vera after her. Somewhere up on the cliff a car started up. She reached the top of the bar and staggered over the other side, which was steep. She lost her footing and fell. Sanducci appeared against the sky above her. He didn't see her. He was crying and hugging his box. She lay very low, watching.

At the far end of the beach the servicycle started back. It had a faintly different sound from the lightweight machines. A searchlight played over her. Its probing light caught Pedersen sitting in the saddle, with his legs on the ground, idling his engine and peering round him for the others. A shot echoed over her head. Pedersen gunned the hell out. The searchlight moved on.

The patrol cops still hadn't gotten down the cliff. A police car had driven to the edge of it, though, and its searchlight was the one sweeping back and forth across the beach. The fog was very low. It wasn't more than five or six feet high now. A cyclist came whirling through the surf, and the searchlight caught the spray behind him. He skidded, righted himself, and swept by her. She heard Pedersen shout. Pedersen was trying to round them up for the getaway. The searchlight hit her. She waited until it passed on, got up, and ran again. She was right in the middle of whatever rendezvous Pedersen was trying to get together. In the darkness two cycles whizzed by very close. The noise seemed to come from every side. She didn't want to be hit.

Somewhere in the darkness, very close to her, she heard Sanducci crying. The searchlight swept back again and caught him. He stuck his arms up into the air. "I surrender," he said. "I surrender." Nobody heard him. He walked down the searchlight beam, waving his box.

Maybe he thought he could ransom himself.

None of the cycles except Pedersen's servicycle had a muffler. Either another shot rang out, or one of the motorcycles backfired. It didn't make any difference to Sanducci. He waved his arms harder and screamed at the top of his lungs. He began to run towards the cliff.

Allie lost her head. She could hear the cycles closing in. Maybe they wanted to finish her off first. She got up and ran straight for the surf.

Another cycle appeared. It was Purvis. He was singing to himself, not words, but just crazy syllables. He was having trouble keeping the cycle up in the surf. Just as he had it balanced it would wobble, or a wave would wash against it. He was headed right for her, and he didn't see her.

Pedersen appeared out of nowhere, and switched on his beam. It hit her. She froze.

But it was too late. Purvis was doing sixty. He clung on to the handle bars and leaned back. The cycle reared up and hit her in the groin, just as the searchlight swept over them again. Pedersen cut his beam.

She fell face forward in the water, with the cycle on top of her. Purvis sailed free and fell with a splash. Pedersen came up behind and yanked him up, somehow swinging him on the servicar behind. He hit with a loud metallic swack. Pedersen took off down the beach after the others.

Janey had seen it all. She ran down the bank to the edge of the water.

Allie was obviously dead. The cycle had crushed her pelvis, and the handlebars had hooked one of her breasts. The water washed over her open eyes. Her hand still clutched her purse.

Janey didn't have time to feel anything. She knelt down and tried to pry the purse loose. She couldn't. She had to open it right there. She waited until the searchlight swept on after Pedersen. The patrol cops were on the beach now. One headed towards Sanducci. The other went right by her, drenching her with spray.

She lost her footing and fell. The oily, slimy water got in her nose and eyes. She opened the purse when the surf receded. The pictures were there, all right, in a sodden envelope. She ripped it in half, against the tough emulsion. Then the emulsion tore more easily. She threw the scraps one by one into the water.

It was only then that she noticed that she was sitting up to her waist in the waves, and that for some inexplicable reason the engine of the cycle on top of Allie was still turning over. The machine kicked like a dying animal. She sat there and watched it.

When Torrey found her she was sobbing. "I got them," she whimpered. "I got them." She didn't want to leave Allie. She had never seen a death before. She didn't believe it.

Torrey led her across the sands and up to the house.

Purvis' long-playing record was still churning on. It had all happened as suddenly as that. It sounded eerie through the rain. It was more alive than he was.

Vera sat on the steps of the porch, with a guard over her. There was a big bruise on her forehead. She was muttering to herself, tonelessly.

There was a sound of cycles, and the patrols came in, shepherding Pedersen and the gang between them. They had their revolvers ready, just in case. Purvis was still sprawled on the servicar, face down. He didn't move.

The record ground on.

"Why doesn't somebody turn that thing off?" asked Torrey. Sanducci sat with his head in his hands. He wasn't a pretty sight. He still clutched his box. Torrey came up and pried it out of his hands. Then he opened it.

He had been expecting money. It wasn't money. Sanducci had grabbed the wrong box. He had got the one Vera used to store the little packets of dope in. Torrey took them out one by one. There were quite a lot of them, and there was no mistaking what they were. They were worth a lot of money, more money than Sanducci had had in the other two boxes put together.

Sanducci stared at it and licked his lips. It was something he'd never even suspected, and now he was stuck with it. No matter what he said, they wouldn't believe him. He began to cry.

There wasn't much point in staying there in the rain. One by one the police began to load them into the patrol cars. They had to carry Purvis and Bob. Pedersen looked down at them. They were his boys. A funny look came over his face. Then he turned on Vera and just spat. He didn't have to do anything more. That was enough.

Torrey drove Janey back to town himself. Of course they'd have to detain her, but the way things had gone, they wouldn't detain her for long. He reached across the seat and squeezed her hand.

THE END